Ellen Macias is an English and reading teacher in the suburbs of Chicago. She is the mother of two boys, Oliver and Gabe, who exhaust her and amaze her in equal measure. They are the greatest joys of her life. When not teaching and hanging out with her boys and dogs, she spends her time gardening, reading, and thinking about exercising.

The First Rays at Dawn

Ellen Macias

The First Rays at Dawn

Vanguard Press

VANGUARD PAPERBACK

© Copyright 2024
Ellen Macias

The right of Ellen Macias to be identified as author of
this work has been asserted by her in accordance with the
Copyright, Designs and Patents Act 1988.

A CIP catalogue record for this title is
available from the British Library.

ISBN 978 1 80016 869 5

This is a work of fiction. Names, characters, businesses, places,
events and incidents are either the product of the author's imagination or
used in a fictitious manner. Any resemblance to actual persons, living or
dead, or actual events is purely coincidental.

*Vanguard Press is an imprint of
Pegasus Elliot Mackenzie Publishers Ltd.*
www.pegasuspublishers.com

First Published in 2024

**Vanguard Press
Sheraton House Castle Park
Cambridge England**

Printed & Bound in Great Britain

For my dad, who taught me to write.

To all the people who helped this book take shape, thank you for your expertise. From John Sibley Williams's feedback to Natalie Tilghman's editing to the many wonderful folks at Pegasus Publishing, this book would not be without you.

To my early supporters — Peggy Barron, Siobhan Szabo, Amy Christian, and Rita Fischer — who were some of the first people to read this story and told me to keep going. And to Tara Young, for lending her expert eye for one, final read.

To all the women from D128 who have dared to empower me, I am so in awe to be surrounded by your strength and beauty. Each of you is in this story.

To Dan, for building Legos and webshooters with the boys so that I could take this on.

And of course, to my mom, you taught me to always follow through with what I started and you always catch me when I stumble, which, let's face it, is often.

And lastly but most importantly, to my sons, you are the force of nature that urges me forward. I hope that you surround yourself with strong women and that you help to make them even stronger.

Contents

Chapter 1
Cala
Urendia

Wives are a commodity in the Kingdom of Urendia — just as gold or land is — and so my father collected them in much the same way. Despite his position as overseer of the gold mine and a modest house in the village, my father was not an attractive suitor. Few were willing to allow their daughter to be married to a former slave, no matter what wealth he had inexplicably amassed for himself.

So my father did what came naturally to him — he schemed to get a wife. Through his dealings with the mine, my father had come to learn that a respected gold trader, who had thirteen wives and a proud villa overlooking the sea, preferred the company of male courtesans. My father had held onto this morsel of information for quite some time until it might become useful to him.

One evening, he waited in a dark alley until he saw the trader emerge from a courtesan's apartment. He watched as the man pulled a cloak over his head, looked both ways, and took off toward his waiting carriage. It was there that my father intercepted him to make his offer: if the trader allowed my father to marry one of his daughters, he would not share his secret. The trader sent his second daughter from his eighth wife to my father the next day. And this is how my father earned his first wife.

Soon, he procured a second and then third wife in similarly unscrupulous ways. But my mother — my father's fourth wife — was not quite so easily won. My mother, daughter of an innkeeper, would serve the customers at the inn's tavern. She caught my father's eye one night when she dropped an ale at his table. Unwilling to earn her affection by more genuine means, my father set out to discover what he could about the innkeeper. But try as he may, he could find no useful information. Much to my father's dismay, it seemed my grandfather was an honest man who ran a clean business. But he persisted.

My father began to frequent the tavern and would leer at my mother as she worked. He tried his best attempt at flattery, and when that didn't work, he tried offering generous tips — all to no avail. My mother would not be won by this unpleasant patron, and her father would not force her. It must have truly baffled my father that not all men wielded their power in cruel ways just because they could.

This went on for some months until my grandfather, most tragically, fell ill. He was unable to keep up the tavern, and my mother, having to tend to her ailing father, could not continue to serve the patrons. Soon, my mother and her three younger sisters found themselves in a very desperate way. It was a sad sight to behold, the plight of the kind innkeeper and his sweet daughters, but few had any extra coin to offer them. Few except my father.

It was an easy choice for my mother. An awful, sickening choice. But an easy one. My father gave her family the means to settle into a little apartment and keep enough food in the pantry so that no one would starve (not a bit more, you'd better believe). And in return, she gave him her hand.

Before long, my mother found herself with me in her belly, and despite how much she hated my father, she found that she loved me as I grew inside her. She sang me songs about the ocean and knitted me a blanket with blue flowers along its edge. She named me before I was even born, Calandria, which means first rays at dawn.

***

"Get up, lazy girl!" Teetee sticks out her tongue playfully.

I pull my blanket over my face, edging the well-worn blue flowers with my thumb, a comforting habit I developed before my first memory. My groan doesn't dissuade my Aunt Tetunia, or Teetee as I have called her since I could make sounds, as she walks over to our bed and pulls the blanket off of me.

"Teetee!" I groan again.

"Cala, if you do not get up this very moment, your brothers and sisters will surely have eaten your share of breakfast."

"I'm up, I'm up."

Teetee smiles at me, her round face full of warmth. She has already tucked her brown hair back beneath a scarf and pulled her apron tight over her tunic, ready to get the day's work underway.

I make up the bed that Teetee and I have shared for my fifteen years of life then splash water on my face from the basin. Teetee attempts to run a comb through my wavy, auburn hair, and I squirm while she braids it.

"Just like your mother's, sweet girl," she says often. "Deep red like the changing leaves."

She says it to keep my connection to my mother alive, but it always makes me sad. I have my own ways to feel close to her, like the final step of my morning routine. I lift my mother's pendant from the window sill, kiss it, and put it on. *Good morning, Mamma.*

After securing the necklace around my neck and dropping the pendant underneath my tunic, I make my way into the courtyard where food is sprawled on the table. The mothers tend to serve the children food outdoors whenever possible. "Better the birds clean up after you hellions than me!" Teetee admonishes us in her playful way. Fine by me. I cherish every moment in the sun.

Children swarm around me, some finishing the last bits of their bread and jam. Others erupt in the few moments of play that the mothers allow before the day gets underway.

My father's children can be divided neatly into two camps: those who are obedient to him, and the rest of us. My father's first and second wives — servile in their own right — did their best to raise their children that way. They were largely successful, save two unwieldy souls: my half-sister, Sentaya, and my half-brother, Rayon.

Sentaya and I were born the same year, only a week apart, and crawled and then walked and eventually ran beside each other whenever we could. Rayon was two years younger — thirteen to our fifteen — and took to following us around once he was big enough.

"Did your mother even bother braiding your hair this morning, Sentaya?" I ask, smiling at the thought of Sentaya's mild-mannered mother struggling to subdue her willful daughter.

"She tried," she says with a smirk, not looking up from her task, which appears to be sharpening a stick with a knife beneath the table, where her mother would not be able to see.

She hisses between her teeth as she brings up her hand, blood forming along her palm where she cut herself with the knife. She tears a piece off the hem of her tunic, wraps the wound, and goes right on sharpening.

Rayon laughs and shakes his head. "It would take a good deal more than a braid to tame that wild one."

"Oh, hush," says Sentaya from beneath her mane of hair, but I can hear the smile in her voice.

"And how about you, brother?" I turn to Rayon. "What adventures are brewing in that mind today?"

"One in which I summon a charm to turn my loathsome tutor into a donkey, so that when he tries to teach us our equations, all that comes out is a heehaw." We all laugh. "Could you imagine the look on Master Gregor's face when he tries to call me a hopeless idiot and instead brays like a useless ass?"

"I think you might earn the beating of a lifetime from Father," I say.

"It would be worth it," says Rayon, staring off as if lost in his magical moment. "Just to never have to hear that man's voice again."

"Breakfast is over!" The call of Sentaya's mother freezes the motion of the courtyard, and the children trudge off to their morning activities: the girls to their chores and the boys to their schoolwork.

We Sida children are confined to our chores and schoolwork for most of our days, but we manage to find moments to get lost in play. Even now, adolescence dawning, we still slip back into our childhood games every now and again.

Rayon's favorite game is mountain expedition, where he leads us to the summit of the stone table of the courtyard, waving our flag made of purloined linens wrapped around a tree branch while Rayon cries out, "We declare this summit in the name of the Kingdom of Cressida!" Cressida is the secret kingdom that we created by starting with the first letter of each of our names and ending with our last name, 'Sida'. The crest is a sun with three rays, one for each of us, and the circle in the middle for Teetee. We agitate their mothers to no end by carving our crest onto tree trunks, underneath tables, and even once into the wall. It was made clear to us with the wooden kitchen spoon on our rear ends that we had crossed the line on that last one.

Sentaya's favorite game is wild ponies, which doesn't have a particularly clear objective. We just gallop around the yard, unbraided hair bouncing with each step we take. Rayon, whose hair is cut short, shakes his head dramatically as if long locks flow behind him, sending Sentaya and me into fits of laughter.

My favorite game is school. I love nothing more than pretending to read and write and learn about the world. Recently, Rayon's mother, Brena, discovered me playing teacher with Ramon and Sentaya seated cross legged on the ground before me. She whipped the back of my legs with a silberry branch. "Learning is not for girls," she said firmly when she was done, her worn, sagging face betraying no emotion as a strand of her graying hair slipped from her tight bun.

My father looked on with approval. He would have order in his household, but sometimes I think he relishes the moments we defy it, as he never seems more satisfied than when one of his children must be forced back in line.

But today, our play will have to wait. The girls have a household to run alongside their mothers, and the boys have lessons to attend to, even if they'd rather their tutor was a donkey.

"Come on, sweet girl," says Teetee, wrapping her arm around my shoulder and pulling me into a sideways hug. "It's market day."

My father's third wife, my Aunt Tetunia, does not have any children of her own. She is barren, of which he reminds her daily, calling her a broken thing or a useless woman, sometimes issuing a kick or shove for good measure. Any time he comes into the room, she bows her head and slumps her shoulders. When I was young, I found myself pitying her gesture of submission. Now that I am older, I see it for what it truly is: an act of deception.

My father won Tetunia more easily than the rest. She was the sixth daughter of a street sweeper who spent every last coin on the drink. When my father knocked on his front door to ask him about marrying one of his daughters, he hesitated long enough only to spit a wad of mucus on his earthen front stoop, call to one of his daughters from within, and give her a little shove toward her new husband. "Get you gone, girl," were his parting words as he slammed the door, accepting a sweaty fistful of coins as the price for his daughter. He hadn't even negotiated.

And of course, my father's fourth wife was my mother, who left this world as I entered it. The sad irony is that she named me 'first rays of dawn', only to plummet into darkness as I was born. I wanted desperately to blame my father for her death, but Teetee has assured me many times that nothing could have been done. I was born on the night of a full moon, and the midwives were spread around the city delivering many babies that night. They had been summoned but arrived too late to save her. Sometimes, when the longing for my mother becomes too great to bear, I cry into Teetee's soft chest, and she tells me how my mother's soul brushed up against mine as I came into this world, kissing me on the forehead and leaving behind the faded birthmark under my hairline that only Teetee knows of.

So, my Aunt Tetunia raised me as her daughter. It was Teetee who told me all about my mother, about the tavern, and the way my father had forced her hand. She told me how much my mother loved me and how much she still grieved her death.

And as far as my obedience to my father? Well, that is not how Teetee raised me.

***

That night, Teetee strokes my hair as moonbeams dance across our bed.

"Tell me a story, Teetee."

"Would you like to hear of the all-women band of pirates who dressed as men when they attacked ships and ravaged towns?"

"No, not that one, Teetee. The one about the queen."

"That one again?" she sighs through a smile, for she must have told me a hundred times, but only because it was her favorite, too.

"Once there was a king who ruled with a heart of stone and fist of iron. He was cruel when cruelty wasn't needed, and his subjects came to hate him deeply. But no one hated him more than his own wife, who saw his cruelty up close.

"One day, the king's eldest son returned with his hunting party, a doe draped around his shoulders.

"'A doe?' The king spat into his son's face. 'And just what am I supposed to do with a doe?'

"'You can feed your household, Father.'

"'Feed my household? What do I care if my household is fed when my trophy room is in need of a ten-point antler?' And with that, he struck his son with the back of his hand, sending him staggering backward, dragged down by the doe still slung over his shoulders.

22

"But what the king did not see — or did not care to see — was his wife watching from a castle window overlooking the courtyard. She took in the indignity of her son, sprawled upon the deer carcass, clutching his eye where his father had struck him. And she seethed.

"'Enough,' she said to no one through gritted teeth. 'It is enough.'

"And before her husband and his entourage returned from the courtyard, she hurried to his trophy room, and with hot rage pulsing in her ears, she ripped his insufficient eight-point buck antler from the wall.

"Then she waited. And when her husband staggered to bed late in the night, she lay perfectly still. When she heard his breathing slow and thicken to a snore, she leapt on top of him and stabbed him with each of the eight antlers until every last drop of cruelty was drained from his body.

"'It would seem eight-point antlers are sufficient after all, my king.'

"And while the crime was punishable by death, all they did was bow. Yes, because they hated the king, and they were glad to see him gone. But more so because they saw her eyes alight with a fierceness that bent them to their knees."

"And was she a cruel ruler, too, Teetee?" I ask, even though I could recite the ending having heard it so many times.

"No, sweet child, she was not. But she hung the bloodied antlers above her throne so that all in the kingdom and beyond knew the fierceness inside of her, and the lengths she would go to rid the world of cruelty."

"I wish that she was our queen, Teetee."

"As do I, sweet child." And then she whispers what she always does as I drift to sleep, "You are brave, my girl, and the world is yours for the taking."

***

Sometime in the night, I wake up with a start and reach out for Teetee, only to find the space beside me cold and empty.

"Teetee!" I call out in a panicked whisper as I clutch my blue flower blanket. "Teetee!" I dare to call a bit louder.

I am about to swing my legs over the side of the bed in search of Teetee when the door opens.

"Hush!" she whispers urgently. "I'm right here. You'll wake your father."

"Where were you?"

"Never mind, sweet girl. I'm here. Now that you're up, what do you say to a writing lesson?"

In a few stolen moments here and there, Teetee has slowly taught me the entire alphabet and now we are moving onto small words. It is strictly outlawed for women to learn to write, and most obey as the punishment for learning is five years of hard labor for the kingdom. There's no need for it, really. Their fathers (or brothers or next male relative in line) sign their marriage certificate, and that's the only document that matters for a woman.

"Do you have any wood left?"

We use the tips of burnt wood as a writing utensil, dragging them across our dirty linens to make the letters. Then, we wash the words away in the laundry, leaving no evidence of our transgression.

Once when we had just started our lessons, my father caught me picking bits of wood out of the cooling fireplace and demanded to know what I was doing. I blurted out that I liked the smell of wood. He muttered that I was a stupid girl and left me to my wood.

Later that night, I'd reported my quick thinking to Teetee, with a proud smile on my face. But Teetee only issued a warning. "Your father is a dangerous man, Cala," she'd warned sternly. "Stay out of his way."

And even though I'd nodded, she'd persisted. "Tell me that you understand."

"Yes, Teetee. I understand."

Teetee would deliver those stern warnings about my father often, her gaze lingering on my face a moment or two after the conversation had ended, as if she could read my future there.

But this night in the safety of our dark room, she issues no warning, instead only looking on with approval at the shapes taking form beneath the candlelight. "Good, your letters are becoming more precise."

I beam into the shadows and practice my letters until the small hours of the morning, when we both succumb to sleep, the smell of burnt wood on our fingertips.

***

I feel groggy as the first shaft of sun pierces through the small window of our bedroom.

"Get up, Cala," Teetee says with a distinct edge to her voice that wasn't there the previous day. "It's ranking day."

I want nothing more than to roll over, curl up beneath my blue flower blanket, and shut out my least favorite day of the month.

For the most part, my father ignores his children, maintaining that child rearing is women's work. He emerges in the courtyard or kitchen at unpredictable intervals to keep everybody in order. Nobody, not even Teetee, dares stray too far out of line knowing that my father might be lurking around the corner at any moment. But mostly, he leaves us to ourselves. The women and girls see to the cooking and cleaning and baby rearing. The boys sit with the tutor who comes each day for their studies.

That is, until ranking day. One day of each month, all household activities come to an abrupt halt, and my father takes a monthly interest in his six children. On this day, the mothers scrub our faces and hair. They put us in our most presentable clothes. We skip breakfast that morning lest we might offend my father with an errant crumb on our clothes or smudge of jam on our faces. Once we are sufficiently prepared, the mothers march us into the courtyard to wait for my father. Though our faces are raw and our bellies are empty, the trepidation we feel is by far the greatest agony of ranking day.

On this day, as the name suggests, my father ranks his children. From what I gather from Teetee, he has ways of collecting information about his children. Between the mothers' reports, the children's tattling, and his own lurking observations, my father pieces together a monthly assessment of my siblings and me. As we huddle in a jumbled mass in the middle of the courtyard, my father walks up to each of us, takes us by the back of the neck, and guides us to our place in line.

You would be right to assume that Sentaya, Rayon and I find ourselves at the end of the line with more frequency than the others. But there have been exceptions.

Once my eldest brother, Thalen, ordinarily unquestioningly obedient to my father, asked him why our house was smaller than others nearby. No sooner had the words left his mouth than my father struck him across the face and sent my brother sprawling on his hands and knees. When ranking day came that month, my brother, his cheek swollen, found himself at the end of the line.

Another time my sister, Nenune, a meek, trembling little thing, had burnt the baked fafulli when my father hosted a business associate for dinner. When we saw the black-crusted edges of the dish come out of the wood oven, we knew what was in store for Nenune. She shook so violently I thought she might drop the dish.

But more often than not, it was one of us three wildlings who found ourselves at the end of the line. It might be Sentaya's careless play or Rayon's neglected schoolwork or my rude comment to one of the mothers.

And as for the punishment, my father dug into the depths of his dark heart and invented something that would torture his children in a way that he understood with terrible clarity. No one can talk to you for the entire month until the next ranking day. Not your mother, not your siblings, and certainly not your father. You live as an outcast within the household for the month. I can't say whether the shame or the isolation is more difficult to endure.

I've had years where my family couldn't talk to me for as many months as they could. Of course, my father can't prevent Teetee from whispering in my ear in our bed at night. On those nights, her words are precious drops of water on cracked lips and parched tongue.

Sentaya, Rayon and I have found secret ways to break my father's rule. Years ago, we invented a small act of rebellion, whispering, "For the Kingdom of Cressida", as we walk by one another, and it is a wonder how that whispered phrase could embolden me to endure another day of silence from my family.

On this particular ranking day, we stand in the courtyard waiting for my father. The cuts on the back of my legs from the silberry branch, issued by Sentaya's mother for my game of school, are still healing, and I find a sliver of comfort in the fact that I know it is coming. When I feel the violation of my father's hand on my neck, guiding me to the end of the line, I stare at my feet and vow I won't cry in front of him.

That night, when the tears are flowing freely, Teetee holds me against her soft chest and smooths my hair.

"That's all right, sweet girl. That's all right. Not your father nor anybody in this world can put you at the end of the line."

She holds me until I cry my last tear, and then we settle into whispered conversation.

"Teetee, are you sad you never had any babies of your own?" I ask her at some point in the night.

"Course not. I have you, sweet girl."

"I know, but it's different. Do you ever wish you could have had a baby that came from your own body?"

"No, Cala."

I think about that for a few minutes, trying to take in her words. And maybe it is because she takes pity on me as the last in line, or maybe Teetee just needs to tell someone, but after some time, she keeps on talking.

"I'm not broken, and I'm not empty. It's on purpose, Cala."

I try to make sense of that, but such things are still beyond my years. So she puts it more simply.

"There's an herb, Cala. It stops me from bleeding."

It still isn't quite simple enough, so Teetee explains it all to me. How women bleed and men sow seed and how a baby results from it all. But Teetee had decided from the day that her father pushed her from his house, the day that she went from one vile man to another, that her body would be her own. And try as he might, she would deny her husband the satisfaction of using her body to produce his child. This would be her rebellion.

She has never told a soul, save the midwife who supplies her with the herb, and she makes me swear I will keep her secret safe. Then she makes me swear again.

And as I start to see Teetee for who she truly is, the pity I once had for her begins to give way to admiration.

***

During that next month, as the wounds on my legs heal, the shame of being last ranked only deepens, and something begins to take root. It is a fledgling thing at first. In flickering moments, my sorrow is overshadowed by doubt and soon anger.

Why should I be last in line? For deigning to want an education? If only he knew that I can write!

And soon, a thought begins to grip me. In the absence of conversation, it becomes my constant companion.

He should know that I can write. Then he will see that I can be educated, that I am equal to my brothers.

Teetee's message echoes through my thoughts. The world is mine for the taking. But I don't want to be the pirate, donning a disguise, hiding her true identity. I want to be the queen — the daring, treacherous queen. I want my father to see me for who I am. And I know exactly how I will do it.

And so it is, with the misguided zeal of a fifteen year old, that I am about to make the worst mistake of my life.

That night, I wait until Teetee falls asleep, then slip out of bed and tiptoe down the hall, pausing every few steps to listen. Slowly, I make my way to my father's office. Terror is pulsing through me, and it is almost enough to stop me. Oh, how I wish it had.

But I push on. I will be brave like the queen. I will be brave like Teetee. Of course, I would later understand that I, as children are wont to do, am mistaking bravery for foolishness, but my young mind fails to grasp the difference. So, I slink to my father's desk, find a piece of paper and ink, and in my best writing, I scrawl a letter:

Dear Father,
I wish to learn.
Yours,
Calandria

I waver for a few moments, but ultimately, I see it through. He would see how capable I am, how determined. I imagine him discovering the letter in the morning, a look of pride coming over his face. No, maybe not quite pride, but at least understanding, understanding that he should not overlook his daughter. I imagine him coming into the courtyard, and asking me, "Is it true? Can you write?"

I scurry back to bed, pull the covers over me gently so as not to wake up Teetee, and drift off to sleep, full of deluded imaginings.

At some point in the night, my father storms into the room, charging toward me until his head jerks toward the empty spot where his third wife should be.

"Where's Tetunia?" he shouts.

Still groggy from sleep, the memory of what I have done slowly materializes, and an unspeakable dread grips me.

"WHERE IS TETUNIA?" he screams. And there is something about the way he says it that feels like the beginnings of a fissure webbing through rock. Yes, there is undeniably anger. But there is something else. There is the desperation of a man who is just starting to understand that he is losing his grip — or perhaps that he has never had one at all — which of course, only leads him to grip tighter.

He grabs me by my hair and drags me out of bed, down the hall, and into the courtyard.

One of the mothers materializes in her nightgown, maybe Craya, but I can only register the silhouette of a plump form. "What is going on?" her meek voice sputters from the shadows.

My father ignores her, and still gripping my hair, twists my head so it turns up towards his. He spits down at me through gritted teeth, the spittle landing inside my mouth. "Where. Is. She."

I truly do not know, and even if I did, I'm not sure I could summon the strength to utter words in this moment.

It doesn't matter. The damage is done. He will wait for her, and he will discover that his grip on his third wife has been nothing more than an illusion.

***

So we wait, my father on the bed, and me on the floor, curled into a tiny ball in the hopes that I might just disappear. Finally, when Teetee sneaks back into our room, she finds my father sitting on our bed, waiting for her.

"And just where is it that you have been, Tetunia?"

Teetee does not cower. She does not droop her head or slump her shoulders. She looks my father square in the eyes when she says, "No doubt you'd love to know."

His fury is unleashed, and though I am curled on the floor with my hands over my ears singing a song about the sea, I cannot drown out the rhythmic thump, thump, thump of my father trying to seize back control.

Some minutes or maybe hours later, it stops, and he drags Teetee away. I hear the front door open, and unfamiliar voices come into the house. In a moment, I begin to understand what was happening. My father is turning Teetee over to the authorities.

I lay awake for a long time before sleep carries me away. At dawn, the sunlight spreads across the floor where I am still curled up. I wake up, confused at first as to why I am lying on the floor. There is a brief, mocking moment where it feels like a normal morning, one where I will soon hear Teetee's playful voice. "Wake up, lazy girl!"

But then the memories come in waves. The letter. My father. Teetee. And the weight of what I have done settles in, and I wretch right there on the sunlit floor. Having emptied the contents of my stomach, I lay there for some time.

Eventually, my door opens, and I think maybe Sentaya or Rayon or even one of the mothers has come to tend to me. But then I remember that I am last ranked this month, and I know they wouldn't violate my father's command. And as I am swallowed by his vast shadow, the realization of who it is takes hold.

My father's gravelly voice cuts through the silence. "Prepare yourself. You are leaving."

"What? Where?"

"You have broken the laws of the kingdom. The penalty for a girl learning to write is five years of hard labor. You are lucky that your father is the overseer of the gold mine. I have arranged for you to serve your sentence there."

As if out of self-preservation, my body can no longer take in its surroundings. My hearing dulls and my vision blurs. I can no longer feel the hard floor beneath me. I'm not sure I would make it through the next part had my senses remained intact. I have a vague sense of being ushered out of the house with a hand gripped tightly around the back of my neck. I recall figures in the hallway, watching me go. I hear a small voice say, "For the kingdom of Cressida", before it is stifled by what must be a hand slapping a face.

I do not know how my feet step one in front of the other, but somehow they do. I cannot tell you how I am brought into the mine or shown to my new living quarters or guided down into the mine or put to work shoveling discarded stone, but somehow that all happens.

It isn't until that evening as I sit dazed on a pallet on the floor that a most unexpected sound coaxes my senses back to life.

A gray-haired woman with lines etched deep into her skin sits on the pallet in front of me, cupping my face into her two hands, and says softly, "Hello, granddaughter."

Chapter 2
Elina
Arcalia: Twenty-two Years Earlier

The Offering divided life in Arcalia in two, like a rip through paper. Before, the families were whole. Their hearts were whole. Afterward, everything was left in pieces.

It wasn't really an offering. That's just what the king called it, and so that became its name. But an offering is a warm meal to a guest. It's a hand extended to someone in need. No, this was no offering. This was theft. Worse. It was kidnapping.

When my parents, like all of the families in Arcalia, were told to offer one of their children as payment for the king's debt, there was no choice for them to make. They only had my older sister, Pru, who was sixteen at the time. My mother said losing her daughter was an agony worse than childbirth — and that nearly killed her. But instead of it feeling as if her body was being ripped apart, it was as if her soul was.

The Offering destroyed everyone a little differently. After all, how does one carry on in a world knowing her most precious thing, her child, could be snatched away at any time?

For some, the grief consumed them entirely. They withdrew from the world, and tragically, they lost whatever children they had remaining as well because they could not pull themselves from their grief to parent them.

Others clung to their remaining children as if they were their very lifeline, desperate not to lose them, hysterical even. Children were locked indoors, kept in cellars, shut away from the world entirely so they could not be taken.

But for my parents, another thing entirely happened. Knowing they could not survive the loss of another child, they turned their next child into something that could never be taken.

***

After my sister Pru was taken, my mother became one of the many who descended into grief. She sat herself in front of the east-facing window, staring at the stone path that my sister last stepped upon as she was escorted away. She kept this vigil day and night for months. My father could do nothing to coax her from that chair.

Ultimately, it was our meadow at the base of the mountain that saved my mother. The green shoots forcing their way through the thawing ground and the smell of damp earth coaxed her from her spot by the window. She would tell me many years later that walking barefoot through the meadow was the closest she could feel to Pru, and so she took up her vigil amongst the wildflowers and grasses, walking in a daze.

Eventually, she slowly returned to life, or at least as much as she ever would. Although I had nothing to compare it to, I've always sensed that my mother used to be someone else, that by the time she had me two years after they took Pru, she was a shadow version of her former self.

She told me she brewed herself a mug of thustle tea every single day during her pregnancy with me, warmed by the knowledge that with just a few sips, she would be childless yet again. And every day she let it cool and ultimately dumped its contents back into the soil. She couldn't bear the thought of having another child, she said, knowing that she might again face an unbearable loss. But she also couldn't end her pregnancy, ushering in that very loss by her own hand. So, she resolved that she would have me. But more fervently, she resolved that she would turn me into something that could not be taken from her so easily.

***

While I was needed on our farm most months of the year, the winter months became what we called the training months. Every year, my mother devised a

39

different way to train me, to sharpen me so that I could protect myself against any force that would do me harm.

The training months commenced the winter I turned five. My mother began by teaching me the uses of various herbs and plants, but unlike my sister, whom she trained in the way of healing, my mother trained me in the way of harming.

I learned that holly hox leaves can be left to soak in someone's tea for a mere minute, and that first sip becomes their last. I learned that bera berries, when dried and ground into a fine powder, can be slipped into someone's food, sending them into a deep sleep. I learned that the liquid from rusard root can be extracted and used to blind someone.

My mother taught me how to identify and employ a whole range of natural weapons. And while I enjoyed these botanical lessons with my mother, who was generally sullen and withdrawn, I was too young to comprehend the lesson that she was really teaching me: the world will hurt you, and you'd best be prepared when it does.

The winter of my sixth birthday, my mother decided I was old enough to be sent off for training. This would be the first of many such stints, where my parents would pay for my training at the hand of any number of experts. First was a bladesmith named Cruck, who taught me how to use a halfmoon knife both at up-close and long-distance range. We practiced on pig carcasses left over from a nearby farm. The network of scars along my hands and arms remind me to this day of my time with Cruck.

At the age of seven, my mother sent me to stay with a slave trader who trained his slaves for the fighting ring. Each day, we were thrown in the ring with a new challenger, whom we fought with our bare hands. The fighting began with the command, 'engage', and continued until we heard, 'disengage'. While I was the smallest challenger in my age group with the least amount of experience, what I found the most tortuous about those particular training months was that you never knew how long the match would last. It was up to the whim of the trader to start and end the fight, so I'd have to defend myself for seconds or minutes or — in one particularly brutal match — over an hour. I adapted quickly, shaving my head so that my hair couldn't be pulled and letting my nails grow long as a way to protect myself. Ultimately, I learned to use speed to my advantage against larger and stronger opponents, but that didn't spare me a broken nose, several broken ribs, and many, many cuts and bruises.

When I was eight, my mother hired a driver to take me into the countryside. I rode blindfolded in the back of a carriage for a day before he dropped me in the woods, saying, "Now find your way home". I nearly died from the cold that first night. But I didn't. And when I awoke the next morning, it was rage alone that fueled me. I would find my way home so that I could unleash my fury on my mother, who would sooner kill me than lose me. I learned to travel at night so that I kept moving when it was coldest, using the stars to guide me home. I knew which plants to avoid, thanks to my mother's training, so I was able to survive on roots and berries that I knew wouldn't kill me. It took me over a week to find my way home — three days alone to find my way out of those woods. And while I had rehearsed the tirade that I would release upon my mother, when I walked in, she looked at me with the slightest twitch of a smile and nod of approval. And instead I said nothing, just turned toward my room and collapsed onto my bed

Perhaps the most surprising training came the winter of my ninth birthday when I learned to read and write with one of the king's scholars. I knew my basic letters and words, but I spent those dark winter evenings reading long manuscripts that he'd bring home from the king's library then copying them, word for word, page after page. When I returned home, the only explanation my mother offered was, "An educated woman is a powerful woman". In all honesty, I preferred hurling knives at pig carcasses, but by then, I understood that it was best to keep my opinions to myself.

As the years wore on, I learned where to lodge a dagger to exact the most lethal blow, how to hit a moving target with an arrow while riding full speed on horseback, and how to defend myself against an opponent while bound and gagged.

I spent the off-season — as I had come to think of the months at home — helping around the farm while continuing my training in any way that I could. A garden hoe became a javelin. A barn rafter, a chin-up bar. And a pig, a wrestling partner, though not always a willing one.

Once, when I was fifteen, a tax collector came onto our farm, looking for my father and his bag of coins, but finding me instead, raking hay in the barn. He wasted little time before he tried to pin me against the wall and force his hand underneath my tunic, an act that was not unheard of. Many tax collectors believed they were entitled to collect more than taxes. Within moments, I twisted his body around until I dislocated his shoulder. He ran from the barn, howling in pain. Of course, he couldn't report what had happened — both because he would implicate himself and reveal that he had been bested by a farm girl.

In the barn afterward, I registered the emotion coursing through me. It was not fear, not in the least. I had wanted to hurt him. And the power that I felt was energizing like nothing I had ever experienced. It took a great deal of restraint for me not to pursue him, to beat his face bloody, to kick him until I felt his ribs crack.

It would seem that, despite the varied and extreme training, my mother's goal was not realized. She had not merely produced a young woman capable of defending herself against those who would do her harm. She had created a weapon ready to unleash itself upon the world.

***

During that same summer, I received an invitation to The Assassins' Guild. I had discovered a slip of paper tucked — most disconcertingly — neatly to the elbow of my tunic sleeve one evening after I had been at the market. Perhaps even more shocking than the location of the note was the message itself.

You have caught the eye of The Assassins' Guild. Come to The Salted Boar when you are ready.

In the months that followed, my mind often wandered to an imagined life in The Assassins' Guild, but I had no real intention of pursuing it further. That is, until my mother announced that my training had come to an end.

It was the winter of my sixteenth year that my mother considered me sufficiently trained. This was no coincidence; it was the age my sister was when she was taken. For my mother, this had become a sort of deadline, and my whole life had been a countdown to my sixteenth birthday, when they would come for me as they had my sister.

"It's done, Elina," she said. "I take pity on the man who tries to take you."

"No," I said flatly.

"What are you saying?"

"I am saying that it is not done. It has not even begun."

Her eyes widened as she took me in, as if just now seeing me for the first time. As my father entered the kitchen, my mother and I stood at opposite ends of the table.

"What's this about?" he asked.

"Elina refuses to stop her training."

"But why? It can finally come to an end. Your mother is satisfied." The pained look that came across his face was nearly enough for me to stop, to give it all up and to become the dutiful daughter that they so wanted me to be.

But that was impossible now.

"Mother is satisfied, is she? She has sent me off to endure enough broken bones? Enough blows to my body? Enough cold, lonely months amongst strangers?"

"It was for your own good, Elina," my father countered. "Your mother…"

"My mother? What about you! You let her send me off, year after year, to nearly die in a hundred different ways! And now you don't like what I've become?" I was screaming now, years' worth of anger hurling itself to the surface. "You lost Pru, and now you've lost me too, but this time it was you who destroyed me! You made me into this! And now, I am a force that cannot be stopped."

My parents were simply staring at me now, horrified — whether at me, or themselves, or this whole damn world, I could not say.

"I, I am so sorry." It was my father who finally whispered these words, staring down at the floor.

"There was no other way," my mother said in a steely voice, tightening her grip on the back of the chair she held.

"No?" I spat back at her. "Then maybe you should have drunk that thustle tea after all." At this, she turned, walked into her bedroom and closed the door.

Had I known that these would be the last words I would ever speak to her, I might have chosen differently.

"Where will you go?" my father asked.

"I have received an invitation from The Assassins' Guild. Perhaps they can stomach who I have become."

And with this, I turned to leave our home, with nothing but the clothes on my back and the anger in my heart.

***

As I set out from my home that late fall morning, I clung to the strip of paper from The Assassins' Guild as if it was a talisman. The day warmed as my journey stretched on, and by midday my sweaty palm had rendered the words illegible. But they were, of course, inscripted upon my mind.

You have caught the eye of The Assassins' Guild. Come to The Salted Boar when you are ready.

The Salted Boar was a tavern on the outskirts of Galendale where my father and I had stopped a few times over the years on our way home from the market. The tavern had a large wooden door with the outline of a boar etched into it, and as I stood in front of it in the cooling evening air, it conjured memories from many years earlier when I walked in holding my father's hand.

Walking through this door again — now on my own with a very different purpose — felt like a betrayal to my father, who, despite his weakness in letting my mother plot out the twisted course of my life, had always been very loving to me.

But hadn't it been he who betrayed me? My mother had been driven by some deranged view of the world after losing her daughter, but what of my father? Surely losing Pru was torture for him, but he knew what my mother was doing, and still, he let her.

Steeled once again by my anger, I opened the door and let the smoky darkness swallow me.

***

The next step of the plan hadn't actually occurred to me until right that very moment. I knew only the location, nothing else. I made my way to the barkeep, and mustering all the confidence I could feign, stated, "I was given a note to come here when I was ready."

He cocked his bald head to the side and stared at me unblinkingly as he cleaned a mug.

"I have a note to come here," I said again, more boldly.

As he continued to eye me queerly, a response came from the end of the bar.

"Don't go shouting your business to the world now." A cloaked figure gestured with his head for me to come over to him.

I took a seat next to him, and without revealing his face from beneath his cloak, he said, "So you're ready, are you?"

"Yes."

He looked me up and down. "Time shall tell." Then he dropped a coin on the bar, finished his ale in one gulp, and turned to leave.

"Are you coming?" he called back, nearly imperceptibly amidst the din of the tavern.

I slid off the stool and followed the cloaked man out into the darkening evening.

***

The cloaked man approached a black mare tied up in front of the tavern.

"I wasn't expecting to run into you tonight. We'll have to ride double. Oh, and I'll need to blindfold you of course." He held out a black strip of fabric.

I had learned long ago to extinguish any ember of panic before it ignited. Instead, I focused all of my energy on assessing the situation. The man's cloak concealed his form, so I could not fully gauge his threat. But he had a considerable height advantage, and being blindfolded and not in control of the reins certainly didn't help.

I stepped forward. "I'll sit at the back."

"Suit yourself," he said as he tied the blindfold.

I very much liked being underestimated.

My cloaked guide began to whistle a cheerful tune loudly over the wind and hoof steps, perhaps believing this would be enough to disorient me. It would take far more than the loss of sight and sound to let any ember of panic catch fire.

***

The cloaked man slowed his horse with a, "Woah", and a pull of the reins. He dismounted and took my hand to help me down before untying my blindfold.

I blinked as the light from two enormous lanterns cut through the darkness. I had never seen anything so grand as the enormous stone mansion before me, with its two turrets and an archway entrance, save the palace in Galendale, which I had only ever taken in from afar. Now, standing here, feeling altogether swallowed by this castle in its own right, that familiar ember of panic breathed to life.

"Master Sera will see you." The cloaked man nodded toward the front door then guided his horse in the opposite direction.

With a steadying breath and as much swagger as I could muster, I turned toward the front door and strode through the arched entryway of The Assassins' Guild.

Chapter 3
Cala
Urendia

In a single day, I have been dragged from bed by the hair, born witness to Father beating and then arresting Teetee, and finally been cast out from my home, only to become a slave. It seems fair to assume that my world is through spinning around and around for one day. In fact, it is not.

I stare blinking at this stranger on the pallet across from me.

"Your granddaughter? But how…"

"Yes, Calandria, your father is my son. And you are as beautiful as I have always imagined you to be."

"Grandmother," I say, dazed by yet another spin of my world.

"Please, call me Granna. It is what I called my own grandmother many years ago."

"Granna. But how? Why are you here? Why hasn't my father gotten you out?"

"Your father is a very misguided man, Cala. Surely, you must know that."

With the mention of my father, the gravity of what has happened crushes me. I collapse into this woman, my grandmother, and I say through great heaving sobs, "Why? Why did he do this?"

Granna just strokes me and says, "Hush, hush", for some time until, finally, I quiet.

Then, she tips my chin up so that I am looking up at her smiling face, and she says, "Now then, I think it is time you heard your father's story."

She speaks softly to me well into the night, completing the blank pages of my father's story. And while I have spent many hours imagining that story, the truth of it is not something that I could have ever conjured.

***

My father was born in the pitch black of the gold mine. My grandmother was — and still is, it would seem — a slave in one of the most gruesome slave mines in Urendia, where the unfortunates who lived their short lives there could expect no sort of special treatment, even with swollen bellies. They were held responsible for finding themselves in such a way, even when, of course, they were not. The women of the mine had a particularly hard existence, especially the young, beautiful ones, such as my young grandmother.

The slave drivers at least had the mercy, if one would be so inclined to call it that, to allow the pregnant women the job of sorting the gold, picking out the large bits that would be valuable as whole pieces and separating them from the rest. This at least afforded them the small luxury to remain somewhat stationary during their grueling shift in that underground hell.

And so that is where my grandmother found herself when her labor began. She knew the guards would take no pity on her, so she found her way to an empty mine tunnel, and this is how my father entered this world. No light or joy waiting to welcome him, only darkness and misery.

***

My father spent his early years in the mine nursery, although that seems too delicate a word for what it was: a thatched-roofed hut near the mouth of the mine where the mothers could leave their babies when they went down. The proprietors allowed for the babies to be looked after, only because in the long run, it would increase their profits to add to the supply of slaves. Despite the drafty walls and bare earthen floors, the children's early years in that nursery were the most freedom they would experience in their lives. They were allowed to do as children do and were mostly left alone to occupy themselves in play. They saw their mothers in the few hours they had between their long shifts in the mine.

Once the children were old enough to follow directions, they were put to work in the mines. They were useful to fit in small spaces and reach gold deposits that were otherwise inaccessible. My father's time in the mines began when he was not yet five years old. My grandmother managed to keep him in her quarter and would do her best to keep an eye on him. And so it went on, day after day, year after year. This meager existence lasted until the day after my father's eighth birthday.

***

It was a sunny spring morning when the first blossoms sprouted to life on the dormant tree branches. Of course, the slaves did not feel the sun on their faces nor see the first blossoms sprout to life, but nonetheless, that is where the story finds itself. It was on this unfittingly cheerful morning that the king of Urendia felt a sudden flutter in his heart. Then the flutter gave way to what could only be described as a wildebeest sitting on his chest. His face grew red, which wasn't an altogether unusual sight given his propensity to fly into red-faced rages. So the servants and courtiers carried on around him as he grew redder in the face, clutched his chest, and quite unceremoniously slumped over in his golden throne. It was only then that the stir made its way through the room, and then the palace, and eventually the kingdom at large: the King of Urendia was dead.

While this was a most unfortunate day for the king, it was in fact, the first time in my father's short life that fortune began to smile upon him, or at the very least offer him a wry smirk. You see, this was a heartless king, whose every decision depended solely on how much gold it would provide him. As you might imagine, this led to circumstances like the one at the gold mine, where the slaves were forced to expend every ounce of their lifeblood toward earning profit for their kingdom.

The king's son, however, was slightly less heartless. He had spent his formative years traveling to kingdoms near and far. It was on his travels that he began to see other ways to treat one's subjects. A gentle-hearted queen across the Caspian Sea shared very wise words with the young, future king: a kingdom only reaches its highest height when its lowest subject is treated with dignity. He found himself affected. And while he wouldn't shed the value of profit that his father had so deeply ingrained in him, he would come to believe that such profit did not need to be earned with his subjects' lifeblood. Or at least not quite so much of it.

And so, the new king did not close the mines. But he did enact a series of decrees that would better the lives for the slaves within them. The slaves now worked twelve-hour shifts, which meant that they would have a few hours to themselves before they would crawl into bed at night. No small freedom after years of work and sleep and nothing else. They were fed three square meals a day, and even though one was taken in the black depths of the mine, they found their bellies empty less often than before. As the guard read the list of decrees to the slaves, it wasn't until he read the final one that my father picked up his weary head.

Slaves who show themselves to be especially loyal to the kingdom may earn advancement in the mines.

Now, most of the slaves, including my grandmother, scoffed at these final words. For their hatred of the kingdom was bone deep, and they would pledge no loyalty, even for the chance of advancement. This was the one dignity that they clung to. They may be forced to do the hard labor of a kingdom who had scorned them, but their allegiance would be their own to give.

And oh, how they gave. You might imagine that the blackness of the mines snuffed out every shred of light and love in their hearts, but light and love can persist even in the darkest of places. When a fellow slave was sick or weak, he could be sure to find an extra crust of bread tucked into his hands when he awoke. Or if he found himself keeled over on the floor of the mines, sure he was taking his last breath, he would feel the trickle of water poured onto his lips or perhaps a kind word in his ear, and he would muster the will to go on. And in the evenings, when the sweet relief of sleep beckoned, they stayed up to tell each other stories from their pasts.

And when they had no pasts, they told stories from their minds.

The slaves had nothing to give, and yet, they gave.

There were exceptions, of course, including my father. Despite my grandmother's urging, my father would not share his bread or his water or his kind words or his stories. And what is worse, he was known to turn his fellow slaves over to the guards. To show allegiance to a guard over a slave was the worst trespass a slave could commit. But my father learned that he could earn their favor, and with it, certain advantages. He might get an extra ration of watery soup or crust of bread. Or the first spot in line at the end of a shift, securing for himself the time it took for the long line of slaves to snake toward the mouth of the mine. Or a second pallet to lay on top of his own, so that he almost couldn't feel the hard earth underneath his back while he slept. For my father, these advantages were worth the price of betrayal.

So when he heard this final decree leave the lips of the guard, my father picked up his weary head. And the corner of his lips twitched into the slightest trace of a smile. For a plan was hatching. A way out was materializing. And my father would step on the backs of anyone in his path to follow it. Even his own mother's.

***

Unlike her son, my grandmother had not been born in the mines. She lived her first sixteen years with her family in the nearby kingdom of Arcalia. And thus her heart ached for not one life but two: her lived life and her lost life.

In her lost life, my grandmother had felt happiness. She had felt freedom. And she had felt love. Her family's farm nestled against the Balkin Mountains, which provided shade in the summer and shielded from the wind in the winter. Between their home and the mountain, a field of wildflowers lay like a blanket over the land. Her mother, my great-grandmother, learned the secrets of the flowers and herbs that grew in that field, and she put them to work in various teas and poultices that she would use in her work as a midwife to ease the pain of labor or bring down a baby's fever. Of course, there were other remedies she would provide to young women finding their way to her door on moonless nights, but those were not spoken about.

For you see, by order of the King of Arcalia, it was a subject's duty to reproduce in order to provide subjects to serve the kingdom. Beyond that, it wasn't the king's concern whether a mother could put food in those subjects' bellies or provide a solid roof over their heads or keep them out of a wrathful father's path. It was merely the mother's duty to provide the subjects to her kingdom, and any effort to disrupt that line of production was strictly outlawed.

Therefore, it was at great risk that my great-grandmother would harvest the thustle weed and store it in tiny muslin pouches, which she hid beneath the floorboard. And it was her sworn duty to the kingdom to turn away those young women who found themselves in trouble asking for her help. But she did not.

And so, my grandmother lived a happy childhood, running barefoot through the blanket of wildflowers to collect the ingredients for her mother's recipes. Her mother had taught her rhymes to remember which plant could be used for which ailment.

'A leaf of tumera and root of night's cloak, and you will see the fever broke.'

'The seed of poppy weed finely ground, and your sorrows will surely be drowned.'

She knew the name and function of every living thing that grew out of that soil. She knew it by scent and sight and soft touch against her cheek. She had no siblings, but she was never alone, for the wild things of her mountainside were her most dear companions.

Like the King of Urendia at that time, the King of Arcalia was also a cruel and greedy ruler. But unlike the King of Urendia, he was a foolish one as well. The two kingdoms had been long-time trading partners, benefiting from the various products that each kingdom — or more precisely, their slaves — produced. But the King of Arcalia had driven up a debt over the years, taking more than he was able to return in order to create a lavish palace for himself and his many wives. Finally, the King of Urendia demanded payment, either in gold or in lives.

You might have already guessed which of the two the King of Arcalia found more valuable. Without hesitation, he issued a decree: every family in the kingdom must offer one of their children as a payment to the Kingdom of Urendia. He called it "The Offering." It is a wonder that the grief that consumed the kingdom was not force enough to stop the very sun from shining. The wailing and begging and sheer refusal issued from the hearts of the mothers of Arcalia was, well, there don't seem to be words to describe what that was.

But the will of those in power was carried forth, and a child was taken from each family, by force more often than not. And the wagons of children were carted off to the Kingdom of Urendia as slaves to work in noble households, or in the fields or—in my grandmother's case— in the gold mines. Debt settled.

***

My grandmother nearly did not survive her first descent into that mine. She was used to the bright and free expanse of her field, and the black walls of the mine closed in around her like death itself, threatening to suffocate the very air in her lungs. She would have given herself to it, let the panic and sheer horror overtake her, had her mother's words not echoed in her mind: 'They may take your body, but they cannot touch your heart. Do not forget who you are, my child.' Her mother's words, for better or for worse, pulled her from that near edge of death, and forced her body to take one step and then another and then yet another. This would be the way of her life for years to come. And even when she could no longer remember the sound of her mother's voice, she remembered her words, and she said them to herself often. They may take your body, but they cannot touch your heart.

Well, I knew where the story went from there. My grandmother grew into a young woman and caught the eye of a guard. In her youth, she let herself be won over by the young man. But once their relationship was discovered, he was moved to another part of the mine, and she was left with a swollen belly.

Soon, she gave birth to a son who only knew the black depths of despair, who had never run the wild expanse of a field with bare feet. She could never decide, whose was a worse fate.

Perhaps what broke my grandmother's heart more than anything else was watching her son's heart harden into a wretched thing. He worshipped his own self-interest with more and more fervor, and when he realized this might earn advancement and eventually a way out of the mine, he was willing to go to even greater and more despicable lengths.

"Please, my son," she had begged. "Do not betray—"

"What? These slaves?" He gestured limply to the bodies around him.

"No, my son. Your heart."

He scoffed at the weak woman he saw standing in front of him. Of course, what he failed to understand was that she was stronger than he could ever be.

That night, the King of Urendia threw himself a grand ball to honor his first anniversary as king. My father listened to the music float over the walls of the slave's compound and into his sleeping quarters. By then he was given his own quarters away from the other slaves, as a reward for his most recent betrayal — turning in an old man who sometimes napped during his shift in the mine when his old bones ached and his weary muscles trembled. The old man was punished with a whip, but my father? He was rewarded with his own sleeping quarters. He grinned that first night as he listened to the music from the ball, a welcome change from the weeping and moaning of the other slaves sprawled on the floor around him like animals in the old sleeping quarter. He drifted off to sleep that night, feeling very pleased with himself indeed.

But that would not be his greatest act of treachery. Oh no, my father was far from his lowest act.

***

When my father was a plump infant — yes, even in the depravity of the mines, he was a plump little thing —

my grandmother would have trouble getting him to sleep at night. He would spend his days napping in the nursery, and even though my grandmother was desperate for a few precious hours of sleep, she would take my father out behind the sleeping quarter and walk and bounce and shush, as mothers do. Well, it was on one such night, as she paced the same small stretch of land for what felt like the hundredth time, that the near-full moon shone down on a familiar sight on the ground beneath her feet.

Before she could even understand what she was looking at, her mother's voice echoed in her mind. 'Two sips of the tea with thustle weed will surely, sadly do the deed.'

In that moment, she was overcome with a pang of bitter joy for her mother, her beautiful mother, who taught her every flower and herb and weed. Who showed her the uses that were not spoken about, lest she or one of the young women she helped should be caught defying the king's orders, for denying the kingdom one more precious subject to fulfill its insatiable need for more, more, more. She remembered the young, scared women, many practically girls, knocking at their door in the dead of night, simply asking for 'the deed'. And her mother would pry up the plank of wood on the floor, second from the end, and fetch out a small muslin pouch of dried thustle. No words would be exchanged beyond, 'Two sips of the tea of thustle weed will surely, sadly do the deed'. And with that, she would send them off to choose their fate — and the fate of the tiny seed growing in their bellies.

Here, in the moonlit night, pacing with her chubby son in her arms, she saw it, unmistakable with its waxy leaves glistening in the moonlight. It was thustle weed. And she understood what she must do. She must give the young women of the gold mines the choice to deny the mines one more slave. As she felt her son's soft, warm cheek against her chest and heard his breaths slow as he drifted to sleep, the impossibility of the choice was not lost on her.

She harvested the thustle weed and planted it in various, unsuspecting locations throughout the labor yard. It was slow work as she could only do it under the light of the moon while the night guard dozed. Eventually, the seeds took root and flourished, as weeds do. And before long, the women of the mines knew where to find her and knew to ask for the deed. It was a hard and sad choice, but it was theirs to make. And that was a gift in itself.

After some time, the proprietors began to notice a decline in pregnancies and eventually, a dwindling of births. But they couldn't understand why. Until my father helped them to understand.

It was the one secret my father had kept, evidence, I suppose, that his heart had not hardened entirely, not yet at least. But the fervor of self-interest had taken hold, and my father understood the value of this knowledge. I like to think he hesitated, agonized a bit before turning over his own mother to the guards. But in the end, he did what monsters do. She was sentenced to two years of the hardest labor, which meant longer shifts because she would have to use her own free time to walk, and then crawl, to the deepest depths of the mine to where she now worked. She thought she had understood darkness and suffocation and despair. She realized then she had not. But she was comforted by one thought during those long two years: it was worth it. For the babies who would not meet this fate, it is worth every minute.

***

While my grandmother toiled in the darkest depths of the mines, my father was promoted to his first job outside of them. He was now the runner for his quarter, which entailed running the mined gold from the mines to the collector in a wheelbarrow. No doubt, this was still hard, physical work, but it was hard, physical work with sunlight on your face and fresh air in your lungs, which was no small thing.

While my father's body was busy hauling gold, his ears listened for useful information and his mind schemed. He developed quite a talent for sniffing out the weakness of others and using it to his advantage. It wasn't long before he discovered that the collector for his quarter had a habit of reporting slightly less than what was brought to him from the mines. Another slave might report him, but my father knew that would just mean a replacement and a lost opportunity. No, my father had something else in mind altogether. He gave the collector a choice: secure my father the position of collector or be turned in. My father was soon promoted.

Slowly but steadily, he came to know things, or simply made them up, and through cunning and sheer will, my father advanced. It took many years and what little was left of his soul, but my father made his way up to become overseer of the mine. This meant a great deal many things to my father, not least of which was status and power over the other slaves. But more practically, it meant that he could own land outside the mine and that he could take wives.

***

And so, the blank pages of my father's first chapter are inked in. And with it, a newfound understanding of my father's cruelty.

"He's a monster!" I hiss, as my grandmother's story comes to a close at some point in the early hours of the morning.

"It is easy to see him as such. But you mustn't forget that the light of his childhood was extinguished by this mine. He was born a slave with no father and a mother who could hardly care for him. He barely laughed as a little boy, barely ran or played. To me, he will always be a little boy who was lost to the mine."

"Well, to me, he will always be the father who made me a slave."

"I understand, granddaughter. I understand. But hush now. You must get some rest. Tomorrow will be difficult enough."

And so, I lie down on the scant mat that will be my new bed. Maybe I should pity him for the suffering he endured. But suffering turns people out in one of two ways: it softens their heart to the suffering of others, or it hardens it.

Surely my father's suffering did not need to harden his heart. It did not need to beget more suffering, like the sill worms intent on destroying the argulas in Teetee's garden, until their delicate purple flowers withered and browned.

No, I will muster no pity for my father, suffering or not. I will destroy him. I will loosen his grip on this world until he fades into nothing. For my mother. For Rayon and Sentaya. For Teetee. For myself.

Chapter 4
Elina
Arcalia: Twenty-one Years Earlier

Once inside The Assassins' Guild, I was led through the labyrinth of a manor until I found myself standing face to face with Master Sera.

"I was ready to give up on you Elina." Master Sera offered only this as a greeting. "Sit there." She nodded to the chair in front of her desk.

Her beauty was striking and cold; a pale, angular face framed with plunging jet black hair. She made no effort to smile on my behalf — unlikely, this was a woman who smiled often on anyone's behalf.

"A path suddenly presented itself," I said.

"In The Assassins' Guild, you will learn to forge your own path."

A reply formed in my mind, but I was wise enough to keep that to myself. I glanced on the wall behind her where two crossed swords and words were etched into the stone:

The contract is the only creed. The mark is the only mission.

Master Sera noticed me taking in the words.

"What do you take that to mean?"

"I don't know."

"You will." She paused. "Or, perhaps you won't."

I didn't have much patience for cryptic conversation at this hour of the night, or any hour for that matter, but I focused on keeping my face unruffled.

"The apprenticeship is a year long, culminating in a final opportunity to prove your worth. At that time, you will be inducted into an illustrious guild that has thrived for centuries. Or you will be turned out onto the street."

She let her words settle dramatically before going on.

"If you agree, Ricard will explain the more banal terms of the apprenticeship." Another pause. "Well?"

I took a deep breath and lifted my chin, hoping not to betray the lingering uncertainty.

"I agree."

She ended the conversation by waving me toward the door with the back of hand and returning to her work.

***

On the other side of the door waited a man with a firm, broad body and gleaming brown skin, which I found myself staring at. I glanced quickly back up to his smirking face, and our eyes met.

"Like what you see?"

It wasn't until I heard the voice that I realized it was the cloaked figure that had escorted me here.

"A mild improvement from the cloak," I replied, feigning disinterest. "I hear they let you handle the banal details?"

His grin widened. "Among other things."

"Well, let's get on with it then." It took no small degree of focus to resist glancing back at Ricard's form, lest I might be discovered again.

***

As we toured the manor, Ricard took me to the kitchens on the basement floor, where I would work each morning and evening to earn my keep. Next, came training rooms, a network of open spaces designed for sparring, exercising, and various ways to, 'Improve one's craft', as Ricard put it. I followed him to the dining hall — a grand parlor with a fireplace the size of my entire bedroom at home — and finally, gratefully, the sleeping quarters.

By the time Ricard left me in my room for the night, exhaustion was a palpable weight. It was impossible to believe that I had left my home only that morning, and now, at some hour late in the night or perhaps early into the morning, I had an altogether unfamiliar new life.

Had I not been overtaken by the exhaustion, that ember of panic might very well have engulfed me.

***

What felt like only minutes later, three firm knocks at my door jarred me from my sleep.

"You're wanted in the kitchens," called a brusque voice behind the door.

My mind was hazy as I tried to get my bearings, recalling the events of the evening and remembering where I was. The unfamiliar room had a four-post bed with deep red velvet curtains that could be pulled closed. There was a marble fireplace opposite the bed, which now sat unhelpfully unlit. I shivered from the cold or perhaps the nerves as I approached the wash basin on the other side of the room.

I stood in front of the mirror that hung above the basin, taking myself in. Deep circles sagged beneath my eyes, and my lips were dry and cracked. Two braids limped sadly on my shoulders with my sandy hair breaking free in every possible direction.

Aside from the training months, my mother had braided my hair every morning since I had hair to braid. It was one of the few rituals that we had, and although we never spoke about it, I assumed, like everything else, it was a relic from Pru's childhood. I accepted the comfort of my mother's touch along with the knowledge that it was likely meant for someone else.

But now, in a swift motion, I pulled the knife from my boot and hacked off both braids.

***

After several wrong turns and dead ends, I eventually made my way down the two flights of stairs to the kitchen where I met the backside of a large, aproned woman. She didn't bother turning her head toward me as she shouted, "The dishes are waiting for you in the sink!"

"This is not what I agreed to," I muttered as I found my way to the sink, overflowing with copper pots and pans.

"Most find themselves in a much worse way with a lot less say about it," she called back.

I rolled my eyes. It was far too early for life lessons. "Is there tea?"

"You can help yourself to tea and toast once you scrub those dishes until they shimmer in the stove fire."

Shimmer in the stove fire? I was here to train as an assassin, not take orders in the kitchen.

"And don't think I'm being poetic. Ask the last one. I made her rewash every one."

"The last apprentice?"

"That's the one."

"What became of her? Was she inducted into the guild?"

She turned and faced me for the first time. Her red face plump and shining with sweat beneath the scarf that held back her graying hair.

"Do I look like the bookkeeper? Now get to it. I'll have another batch ready by the time those are done."

I began scrubbing the dishes with the wire brush that was hanging beside the sink, feeling very sorry for myself. Most find themselves in a much worse way indeed.

***

"Hmph," was all the cook offered in praise for my hour of scrubbing, but she nodded toward the kettle, so I figured I earned my breakfast.

"That's just to keep you from fainting, skinny as you are. You'll dine proper with the others, after you clean yourself up of course," she said, eyeing me with surprising contempt for someone who had sweat all the way through her apron. "You can call me Auntie Cook."

"What sort of a name is Auntie Cook?"

"The sort that I gave you. And what is it that I am to call you?"

"Sister Dishwash."

Her look landed somewhere between reprimand and disdain. It's one that I had seen often from my mother — flash of the eyes and curl of the lip.

"It's Elina."

"Well, Elina. Take your tea and toast and then scrub the smell of the kitchen off you. You'll want to make a better impression than that." She paused and eyed my hair. "The steam in here isn't a friend to your hair, I'm afraid."

I reached up reflexively to touch my freshly hacked hair. "Thanks for the confidence."

"They're a pack of dirawolves, mind you."

"Well, I'm sure they'll welcome me into their pack with open arms — or paws?"

"Trick is finding out if it's a pack you want welcoming into." And with that, she turned to finish breakfast, leaving me contemplating my place in the world for a second time that morning. I couldn't decide what would be more tiresome about working in the kitchen — shining the endless stacks of dishes until they shimmered in the stove fire or suffering the unsolicited advice of Auntie Cook.

***

Freshly bathed, dressed in a black tunic and pants that I found in my bedroom, and hair sufficiently tamed, I stood before the double doors of the dining hall. With my hand on the brass door handle, I tried on different facial expressions for my first impression.

"Do they have doors where you come from?" A familiar voice behind me said through an audible grin. "I can show you how they work if you'd like."

I grinned at the door in front of me, despite myself. "Yes, we have doors, Ricard. But none with a roomful of assassins on the other side."

"What's the worst they could do?"

"Assassinate me."

He laughed. "Never on the first day. Come, I'll show you in."

He looped his arm around mine and led me into the dirawolf den.

***

I braced myself for a dramatic halt of the mealtime din as all heads turned toward me.

There was no dramatic halt. Ricard casually led me past the polished wood dining table that stretched the entire length of the room, as I took in the assassins who sat in small clusters or individually, not even bothering to look up.

"You'll need to meet your lead assassin, or lead as we call them," he explained as he loaded his plate with food. "Don't expect a warm welcome. She's about as frosty as they come. Her name is Trina."

"Got it. Lead assassin. Trina. Frosty." I picked up my own plate despite the fact that my stomach revolted at the smell alone.

"After breakfast, you'll spend your mornings in the training hall with the other junior assassins. The trainer is called Smitts. He reports everything back to Master Sera, so show him everything you've got."

"Not sure they'll be able to handle everything I've got."

"Boastfulness doesn't earn you any points around here, so save your energy," Ricard admonished.

"I'll do my best," I said with an eye roll.

"I have no doubts," he smirked back. "After lunch, you are with your lead."

"Frosty Trina."

"Right. That's your on-the-job training, so you'll help her plan and execute any jobs she has."

"Plan? That sounds tiresome."

"A successful job is mostly planning, down to the most minute detail. You'll spend days or even weeks researching, scoping out, planning your moves, and then just minutes of execution. You have to account for everything, so the mark doesn't slip."

"So the mark doesn't slip?"

"The target doesn't get away."

"Got it."

"This is the stuff Trina will teach you. If you can get her to talk, that is."

"She sounds like a delight."

"Probably wouldn't be my first choice of words. Then after dinner, it's back down to the kitchen to help Auntie Cook clean up."

"Ahh, back down to Auntie Cook for more sage wisdom."

"Sometimes I think she's the only one around here who actually knows anything."

I glance up at Ricard to see if he's smirking, but he simply widens his eyes and gives a slight nod in affirmation.

"All right, are you ready to meet your lead?"

"Well, after you've built her up so much."

Now it was Ricard who eye rolled. "Come on then."

He led me to the head of the table, where a slender woman with chin-length hair, dyed purple, sat alone. The two-crossed dagger symbol of The Assassins' Guild was inked on both sides of her neck. Her eyes, furrowed in irritation, locked onto mine in a look that could only be described as, well, frosty.

"Trina, this is Elina, your apprentice," Ricard offered to break the tension. "Try not to be cruel."

"But then I wouldn't be doing my job, would I, Ricard?" she said in a sickly sweet tone.

"Okay then, looks like you two will be fast friends. I'm off."

Ricard joined a small group clustered midway down the table, leaving me alone. I made the mistake of eying Ricard as he walked away.

"Don't waste your time there," she said without looking up from her plate. "You're not his type."

"What, not dark and mysterious enough? Surely, I can work on that."

"No, not male enough."

"Ah, well that I can't work on quite as well, can I?"

She offered not so much as a grunt in reply.

"Listen," I began after a few moments, trying to cut through the awkwardness. "Thanks for taking me on as an apprentice."

"She's making me do this as a punishment. Don't expect any heart-to-heart shit from me. Just stay out of the way, and I won't accidentally kill you on the job."

"I feel inspired already," I said without breaking eye contact.

She held my stare for another moment, sizing me up, before she went back to her plate, and we spent the rest of the meal eating in silence.

***

Towards the end of the meal, Master Sera walked in. Without even raising a hand or saying a word, she garnered instant attention from the thirty or so assassins in the dining hall.

"Those who did not meet quota this month will be summoned today. The rest of you, do not rest on your accomplishments. Failure is but a breath away."

She paused, surveying the room, and somehow, her gaze was as severe as her words. Shame settled into some of the bodies around the room, as they bowed their heads or let their shoulders slump. Ricard was not among the downcast figures, but notably, Trina was — hence, the punishment.

"The contract is the only creed," Master Sera projected across the room.

"The mark is the only mission," chorused the assassins.

With that, she left the dining hall, and conversation slowly resumed. Trina did not so much as glance in my direction before she cleared her plate and left the dining hall.

Chapter 5
Cala
Urendia

While my grandmother — whose name is Prusia but is known as Pru — had never seen me before that first night in the mine, she had her own ways of collecting information. So she knew before she first saw me that her son had sentenced his own daughter to the mines. And she used what little connection she had garnered in her years at the mine to be sure that I found my way to her quarter. And so, when she first saw me, sitting dazed on that pallet, her heart swelled as she took in her kin for the first time. And when she spoke those first precious words and cupped my face in her hands, we each saw a mirrored reflection of our own pale blue eyes.

It is those same eyes that hold my gaze as we prepare to go down into the mines this morning. My senses now fully restored, I am overcome by a near crippling fear as we are marched into the mine.

"The darkness cannot swallow you, Cala. Just breathe in and out."

"I can't see. I can't breathe," I gasp as we go further in and the dusty, jagged walls close around us.

"You can. In... out... in... out..." she says as she lifts and drops her whole body in exaggerated heaves.

I lock eyes with her and follow her command, drawing on some deep instinct to breathe despite my certainty that the air is too thick to choke down.

"Get to the shaft!" A gruff voice cuts through the heavy darkness.

"Come Cala," Granna says, pulling me away from the voice.

She guides me deeper into the mine through a narrow tunnel propped up unconvincingly with eroding logs. We make our way through it, hunched over, until finally it opens to a shaft — no bigger than my bedroom — dug, not in front of us, but down at our feet into the depths of the earth. I glance down into the gaping hole, taking in the excavators already at work, and I am gripped by the understanding that we are to descend down into this hell.

Around the rim of the shaft are stacks of tightly woven baskets, each containing an iron hammer and chisel. She picks one up and tosses it into the cavern below and then descends down a precarious ladder into the hole. I reluctantly do the same.

Finally, we set about to work, using the chisel and hammer to dislodge bits of rock speckled with gold and toss it into the basket. Once it's full, we whistle and a porter comes down to carry out the basket full of rock, depositing an empty one for us to start again. And on it goes.

Soon I have been staring at the same stretch of dusty rock for hours, and the dimly lit cavern wall becomes a blank canvas for my wild imaginings. Sometimes, I imagine Teetee in the stockades being starved or beaten or tortured. Sometimes, my mind takes me back home to imagine my father taking out his insatiable wrath on Rayon and Sentaya. Sometimes it takes the form of memories, and I see myself placing the letter on my father's desk, and I wish I could shake that deluded sense of bravery from myself. I am trapped in a living nightmare.

Thankfully, my mind — sufficiently tortured for the day — lets me savor sweet memories while I sleep: the feel of Teetee's soft chest beneath my head; Sentaya's wild hair, a mane blowing behind her; Rayon's triumphant declaration, "For the Kingdom of Cressida!" as he plants our flag on the stone table. Of course, these memories become torture of their own once I wake and take in my surroundings once again.

But Granna is there, ready to fold me up in her arms. And though she doesn't feel soft and plump the way Teetee does on account of her having given most of her body up to the mines, her embrace fills me with a warmth that I carry with me down in the shaft.

And she reminds me often of the promise to her mother that she has kept all these years.

"They have taken my body, Cala, but they have never taken my heart. And they will not take yours either."

***

A few weeks have passed, and life begins to settle into a rhythm. The pain is still there, but duller, like a stone pressed up against your ribs instead of a knife. Granna says that the pain does not go away. I'm not sure that I would want it to, as it is the last connection to my family that I have.

One evening, Granna says it is time to introduce me to her people. It has not occurred to me that she has people in the mine, but of course she does. She has lived most of her life here.

When we get back to our living quarters after our shift that night, there is a small group of people huddled around our sleeping area. As they form a semicircle around us, I understand that Granna has arranged an introduction.

"This is Willa," Granna says, pointing to a pretty young woman maybe in her twenties, dark eyes and dark hair in a long braid down her back. "She's been here going on eight years now. Ten years hard labor for breach of contract," Granna finishes with a wink.

My eyebrows must rise in confusion because Willa offers an explanation. "Refused to marry my husband. He and my father had already signed the deed, so, there ya go. Breach of contract." That gets a chuckle from the group. I don't quite understand the humor of it.

"Next is Geminara, Gemi." Granna nods to the next woman in the circle, a tall middle-aged woman with her hair shaved clean to her scalp.

She rubs her scalp self-consciously. "I work in the kitchens," she explains. "They shave our heads to keep the jippa bugs out of the food. We sometimes get that around here."

I reach up to touch my head instinctively.

"Don't you worry, child," Granna says. "It's been a good many years since we've had jippa bugs in our quarters. They force the kitchen workers out of habit more than anything." She winks at me. I am beginning to understand that Granna winks a lot.

"This is Abras," she says, moving things along. Abras takes me in, unblinkingly, with his soft brown eyes. He can't be much older than my brother Graniel — sixteen or seventeen if I had to guess. Our eyes meet briefly before we both look away.

"Abras was born in the mine," my grandmother adds, with no further explanation. I notice Abras's eyes make his way back toward mine as we take each other in for another brief moment.

"Lastly, that's Onaris," she says nodding to a man with a gray beard and kind eyes. He tips his head toward me and smiles slightly.

It takes me by surprise, and I notice that I'm frowning a bit, more in confusion than anything else. I have not met many men in my life, just my father, a few of his business associates who come to the house, and the tutor who comes to teach my brothers. But I have never been regarded in this way, acknowledged with such genuine kindness, or acknowledged at all for that matter. I quickly rearrange my frown and nod my head back.

"This is my granddaughter, Cala," Grana says with an unmistakable note of pride.

"Hello," I say shyly.

***

As my time in the mine wears on, the pain is still with me, just as Granna promised. But I know what to expect now, and that is something.

In the mornings we wake up in the darkness of the early morning and wash up as best we can. We gather for breakfast, porridge and weak tea, and we assemble in the mine yard for the counting. This takes some time, but I don't mind. The sun has come up by then, and it's the only time of day we get to feel the sun on our skin.

Once we are all counted and given our assignments, we descend into the mine for the grueling twelve-hour shift, where I take up my spot in the shaft to chip, chip, chip away at the wall in front of me. There's just enough light to see the flecks of gold that shimmer tauntingly in the dusty shadows. Once my body takes over, my mind is free to wander, and most days finds itself trapped in the nightmare of wild imaginings.

The only interruption is our break for lunch, most often a hunk of dried bread, a bit of cheese, and a drink from the common water basin. After the second half of the day — spent in the same way as the first — the bell is rung for the end of the shift. Then we line up and snake our way to the entrance.

By the time we leave the mine, it's long been dark. We make our way to the center of camp to eat our dinner, usually some kind of stew, where the chunks of meat are few and far between. Finally, we settle into our sleeping quarters, where my Granna and her people pull their pallets into a circle on the floor and settle into conversation.

One night, Granna's people tell me their stories. In the mine, one's stories are their most cherished possessions, so to tell them to another is to give a very precious gift. Willa begins.

"When I was sixteen, I fell in love. Well, I thought it was love at the time, anyway.

"My father was a baker, and my job was to travel around the city making deliveries. My younger brother drove the horse, and I rode behind in a pulled wagon, jumping down at each stop to drop the basket of goods to the customers' doorsteps. We started early, much before the sun was up, so my father's rich patrons would have fresh bread by the time they woke up for their breakfast.

"One of our very last stops was a wealthy nobleman, who lived in a grand estate on the outskirts of the city. By the time we pulled up to his house, the sun would be rising, and the members of his household would be awake and moving about the property. One morning, as I dropped the basket at the back door to the kitchens, I saw the most beautiful person I had ever seen. His name was Krister, and the first time I saw him, he was standing next to a fine chestnut horse, brushing his mane and whispering into his ear.

"I must have been staring, because soon a voice called from inside the kitchens, 'Well girl, are you going to leave the bread or not? I've got to get breakfast on the table!'

"The voice of the kitchen maid reached Krister's ears too, and he turned away from his horse and locked eyes with me, still frozen with the basket in my hands. He laughed and said, 'Hello.'

"I was too mortified to respond, so I just dropped the basket on the steps and ran back to the waiting wagon.

"Within a few days, there was a note on my father's doorstep addressed *To the Baker's Daughter*. My father had taught us our letters so that we could read the orders from the bakery.

Next time I hope you'll say hello. My
horse took great offense.
Yours most truly,

Krister
P.S. What is your name?"

Willa paused for a moment, staring past us, as the corner of her lips rose into a slow smile.

"From there it was a force of nature," she started again. "Soon, the few stolen moments during the bread delivery weren't enough, and when I turned to leave, Krister whispered in my ear, 'Meet me by the entrance to the north woods at midnight.' And I did.

"We knew that Krister's parents would never agree to the match — my father's station as a baker was much too low for their son — so we hatched a plan to run away. It was all set. And we almost made it. But somehow his father found out. I never knew how. And he sent Krister away to his uncle in the country before we could even say goodbye.

"As for me, apparently a broken heart wasn't punishment enough. At some point, Krister's father had gotten a look at me and must have liked what he saw. The very next day after he sent Krister away, he knocked at my father's door and gave him a generous offer for my hand in marriage. He was sixty-eight years old, and I would have been his seventh wife.

"It had been a very difficult year for my family. The silt worm had destroyed much of the wheat crop, so my father's bread business wasn't doing well. He had already taken on quite a bit of debt to keep his business. I could hear him and my mother arguing about it most nights. So, the hardship drove my father to accept the offer, and they both signed the contract on the kitchen table that afternoon while my mother wept in her bedroom. I like to think in better times, he might have declined the offer.

"Well, I would have sooner died than let that vile old man touch me, so I ran away to find Krister. I got to the outskirts of the city before I was caught by those cursed guards they had sent after me. You can believe it took three of them to drag me back, one hooked under each of my arms and a third around my ankles. Krister's father said he didn't want a disobedient wife and turned me over to the authorities for breach of contract."

This time there was no smile as she said it.

"I am seven years, two months, and fourteen days into my ten-year sentence. By now I have stopped imagining that Krister has waited for me."

I want to reach for Willa's hand, to squeeze it, to tell her that he will come or perhaps instead that she doesn't need him to. But it seems so insufficient, and I find myself offering only a small nod, for what can really be said to soften such misfortune?

A silence has settled into the group. Somewhere during Willa's story, Gemi joined us, her shift in the kitchens finally done for the night. She sits with her legs pulled into her chest, her arms wrapped around them. My eyes catch on her red, blistered hands clasped around her knees. Granna told me that the guard in charge of the kitchens pours scalding hot water on the slaves' hands if he doesn't think they are working fast enough.

"I suppose I'm next," Gemi says after some time, and I can just barely make out her eyes, heavy with torment, in the flickering lantern that sits in the middle of our circle.

"It's your story to tell," Granna answers warmly.

A few minutes pass, and I'm not sure she'll tell her story, but then she begins.

"My husband, Gregor, was a good man. We married for love, which is a rare thing in this world."

The group nods in agreement.

"Well, not too long after we were married, we had our daughter. We named her Brittania after my husband's mother. She was our world."

Gemi stops to steal herself. Then she goes on.

"It was a bad season for the fever, and Brit fell sick. I paced with her for three days. She just lay there in my arms, and I couldn't get her to take my breast. We called for the midwife, but we didn't have the money to pay for the herbs that would bring her fever down. The midwife told us sadly that she had her own babies to look after, and as much as she would, she couldn't give us the herbs without payment.

"Gregor was an honest worker. Went down every day to the docks to haul fish off those big ships that came in with their catch. He came home smelling something fierce, but to me, he was a prince. Brought home every quint he earned. Never spent a coin on the drink. But it just wasn't enough for any extras.

"By the third day, Brit had grown limp and pale, and we were desperate. That's when the tax collector knocked at our door. Before I knew what he was doing, Gregor hit him over the head with a cooking pan. Not hard, you see. Just enough to knock him out. I think Gregor was just as shocked as I was at what he'd done.

"Gregor untied the collector's coin purse from his belt and took out just what we needed for those herbs for our baby girl. He went to find the midwife, paid her the coins, and brought back the herbs for Brit.

"By then, the collector, who was slumped over in a chair, began to come to. My husband tried to tell him the situation, hoping he might take pity on us, an honest family trying to save our baby girl.

"He did not. My husband was sent to the gallows for attempted murder. They didn't believe a word from his mouth when he said he only hit him hard enough to knock him out. A day later, they came for me."

"But why!" I blurt out, in spite of myself.

"I was an accomplice, they said."

"But you didn't know anything about it!" I insisted.

"It was that tax collector's word or mine. And by then, he had spun a story about how we said we were going to kill him if he didn't give us his whole bag of coins and how he hardly escaped with his life. Never could figure out why, except for meanness and spite, I suppose. And I guess being a little sore about being hit over the head with a cooking pan," she says wryly.

We all managed a smile at that.

"Well, anyway I was able to get word to my sister, and the neighbor said she'd watch Brit until my sister could come for her. My sister's husband has a farm a way out, and there's enough food to go around. I take comfort in that, at least. Brit will be ten and a half when I get to see her again.

"Death was whispering in her ear, that day, I know it was. I miss my baby girl every waking second and the sleeping ones, too, but I'd do it all again just the same way. And I know Gregor would too, may the goddess keep his soul."

With those final words, Gemi curls her knees back into her chest and stares down at the dirt floor in front of her.

No one speaks again for some time. Eventually Abras clears his throat softly before he begins.

"I don't have much of a story. My mother came to the mine when she was pregnant with me. Her crime was finding herself pregnant by someone who wasn't her husband." He doesn't offer any further details, out of respect for his mother, I assume.

"She died when I was seven. Fever," he continues.

"The fever blew in from someplace wicked that winter," Granna jumps in. "It claimed many good souls from us." She nods to Abras to continue.

"Well, Pru looked after me from then on," he finishes.

"And he looked after me," Granna says with a wink.

"My mamma died, too," I offer. Something about Abras's soft voice and sad face urges me to offer some kindness. My hand reaches to my neck to touch my mother's locket out of habit before I remember that my father made me leave it behind.

They all turn to me expectantly, and I realize they're waiting for me to continue to tell my story. And so, I do.

I tell them about how my mother died and Teetee became a mother to me. About life living in my father's house and the monthly ranking. About Sentaya and Rayon and how our laughter found a way. About how Teetee taught me to write, and how I longed to be educated along with my brothers.

I pause. Tears have begun to form in my eyes. I look at their faces, staring back at me with kindness and understanding and love. And maybe it is those faces or maybe it is just because I need to get it out, but I go on.

"But I made a mistake. A terrible mistake. I wrote my father a letter to show him that I could write. I thought that if he could see that, he might let me learn more. I know now it was so foolish. So, so foolish." By now the tears are streaming in earnest.

"But he found the letter, and when he came looking for me, Teetee was gone. I don't know where she was, but he waited for her, and when she came back he hurt her. He hurt her so badly, I wasn't sure if she'd live. But she did, and he turned her in. He sent her to the stocks because she taught me to write. And he only knew because I told him. They took her away because of me."

And then I am folded over myself, sobbing, until Granna lifts me against her and strokes my hair, the way Teetee used to do.

"Hush, child, hush," she says softly. "It isn't your fault. Your father's heart turned against him long ago. I couldn't save him any more than you could save Teetee. Hush, hush." She strokes my hair and rocks me until my breathing slows and my tears stop.

It is Onaris who speaks next. "Cala, there's something about your Aunt Tetunia that you should know."

"Onaris," Granna interrupts. "I'm not sure it's wise."

"She has a right to know," he presses.

After a moment, she nods for him to continue.

"There's something you should know about Tetunia, but I think it will make more sense if I tell my story first."

My head feels jumbled, trying to piece together what Onaris's story could have to do with Teetee, but then he begins, his voice suddenly so low I have to lean in to hear him.

"A good long while ago, I lived with my parents in the slums of Urendia. It was, well, it was not a good place to be a child. It taught me from a young age that there are some bad people in this world. And they would do terrible things to other people, weaker people, smaller people, poorer people, if it meant getting by just a little better themselves.

"For as long as I can remember, one thing drove me forward. I would be their protector. At first, I was just a small thing myself, but as I grew bigger, I discovered I had power of my own. At the time, it was my mother and my sisters who often needed protecting from my father. One day, when I realized that I had grown taller than him, I drove him out of the house. I made it clear that he wasn't to come back, and he didn't.

"Soon, it was other mothers and sisters. Or the boy in the neighborhood with the limp that the other boys would corner. Or my neighbor about to be thrown in the stocks for not having enough coin for the taxes.

"Word spread that I was someone you could call on if you needed help. And wouldn't you know it, others joined up with me, folks who saw that there was a force of good trying to stand up to all the bad in the world.

"Before long, a sort of underground network had formed, and our mission was simple: serve the good people of Urendia. We never officially named ourselves so that we could stay concealed, but we came to be known as The Servants of the People, or more simply, The Servants.

"After many years, we became more organized, and while we still helped the poor folks from back home, we started to understand that to change anything, we had to do more. So we set our sights on the nobility. We knew we wouldn't be able to bring it to its knees, but maybe we could weaken it enough to loosen its hold over the kingdom. We might cut the horses loose on the tax collector's wagon, to delay his work if only by a day. We might pay a lord a special visit to let him know that we had our eyes on him, and he'd better start paying his farmhands their well-earned wages. We might intercept a message dispatched from the king himself, if its content contained harmful decree or damning information."

I take this all in, jaw slack. "I just had no idea. No idea that all this went on."

"I don't suppose you could have. But I imagine you're wondering what all this has to do with you. The Servants had informants in every corner of the kingdom and even inside the palace itself. There were loyal members toiling here in the mines and serving in the king's court. There were men, women, and even children loyal to the cause. Goodwill is abundant, so it seems.

"I came to understand early on that to take a wife would be too great a risk. A wife or children might be used against me should I ever get caught, and I couldn't bear the thought of it. So The Servants became my family.

"Well, one of the most loyal Servants was my good friend named Tobian Greer. He was an innkeep on the eastern side of town. He brought us all kinds of information. You wouldn't believe what people let slip in the shadows of an inn after an ale or two."

He narrows his eyes and searches my face as if for some sign of recognition, but none registers.

"Tobian was your grandfather, Cala, your mother's father. His was the inn where your father first saw your mother. All your father saw was a pretty barmaid. What he couldn't possibly imagine was that, like her father, she was a faithful Servant, too."

"My mother?" I gasp.

"The very same. It broke Tobian's heart in two when he agreed to give her to your father. He was sick, and there were the younger girls to provide for. That was part of it, sure. But once your mother came to understand who your father was, she told your grandfather that she'd be able get The Servants valuable information about the mine, information that could help the slaves there. That may have been true, but I think that maybe she just told him that to make the whole thing easier on him. At any rate, they both agreed that it was for the best, and he signed his name.

"So when Tetunia, or Teetee as you call her, met your mother, she became a part of something much bigger than them both.

"Once Tetunia had earned her trust, your mother shared her knowledge of The Servants with her. She hadn't even gotten through explaining what the whole thing was when Tetunia asked how she could sign up.

They schemed together to use your father's wealth and position in the mine to help the cause. Sadly, your mother died before their plans could come to be, but Tetunia carried on in her memory.

"As for me, I was set up. Not sure by who, but I have my suspicions. That's how I ended up in the mine."

Onaris pauses, and my mind races through the landscape of my memory. But I suddenly don't recognize any of it. During the night, when I would sometimes wake to find Teetee missing from our bed, she was out in the world, helping in any small way that she could. Perhaps sharing information that she had eavesdropped from my father's dealings or passing along a coin or two that she had saved from the market money. And in those small but mighty ways, Teetee had fought to beat back the darkness in this world.

That is, of course, until I got her caught.

As if understanding my realization, Granna pulls me into her again. "You cannot blame yourself, Cala. Tetunia wouldn't want you to."

"Right, there's one more thing," Onaris remembers. "Tetunia sent you word."

He hands me a folded piece of sooty cloth. I unfold it to read the smudged brown letters inside, made perhaps by the charred end of a piece of wood.

Be brave, sweet girl. I will see you again.

***

I wake that night to the sound of weeping close by. It takes me a minute to distinguish dream from reality, but when I am certain that it is real, I sit up and let my eyes adjust to the light. It is Willa, hunched over against Granna who strokes her back.

"What's wrong?" I whisper. Willa lifts her head to look at me, and the moonlight is enough to reveal a red, swollen eye.

"What happened?" I ask in alarm.

"A guard cornered Willa on her way to the outhouse," explains Granna.

"Why?" I ask, still hazy from sleep.

"Because he's a bastard who thinks he can take what he likes," snarls Willa through gritted teeth.

"But you fought back, didn't you, brave girl?" says Granna soothingly, still stroking Willa's back.

"Yeah, this time," says Willa, but her fierceness has given way to something else. Defeat.

"You know you're to wake Abras when you need to go to the outhouse in the night."

"I know, I know," says Willa tearfully. "I just hate to wake him. Everyone is so tired."

"A little lost sleep is worth your safety, Willa," assures Granna, giving her one last squeeze. "Now come, girls. Let's try to get some sleep. Dawn will be here before we know it."

"I'm sorry, Willa." It's all I can think to say.

She offers me a weak smile then lies down on the pallet next to Granna, who continues to stroke her back. I try to fall back to sleep, but the image of Willa being cornered in the night grips me, leaving terror and anger coursing through me. What kind of hell has my father resigned me to? Resigned all of these slaves to? Powerlessness is the ultimate feeling that settles in before sleep finally claims me.

***

Soon, it is my sixteenth birthday. I don't know exactly which day, but Teetee and I had already begun our month countdown, a yearly tradition, when I wrote the letter, so I know it's sometime soon.

My mind pauses for a moment on the memory of my birthdays — where Teetee would wake me up before it was even light out to give me my gift. The thought of it becomes too painful. I decide to tell Granna about my birthday, and she insists we celebrate.

"No need to make a fuss," I say, but I can't help but smile a little. "Well, a little fuss might be all right."

I don't know what kind of celebration is even possible here, but I have begun to see that things in the mine are a little less hopeless than they first appeared.

By now, I've learned that The Servants have been in the mine for some time, but now that Onaris is here, their resolve has strengthened. What was once a general mission to try to protect fellow slaves when possible has become an organized effort to better the lives of the slaves and resist the oppressive force of those in charge.

Each of Granna's people plays a part. Since Willa knows how to write, she is in charge of communication with the outside. She sends and reads notes that help advance various causes. Abras is the ears of the operation.

He's the runner, the same job my father once had. Unlike my father, he did not earn the job through betrayal. He was promoted because of his long legs and unassuming nature. People tend to underestimate Abras, I'm beginning to discover, mistaking his quiet nature for weakness.

A few days ago in the dinner line, an older man grabbed Abras's wrist as he reached for his bread, presumably to take it from him. Before I could understand what was happening, Abras had turned his body so that he was eye to eye with the man and somehow simultaneously twisted his arm around so the man's arm was bent backward in pain.

"Kindly unhand me," he said to the man in a low voice without a hint of fear. And the man did.

I watched the scene unfold with a sense of awe and something else that I can still not quite describe. I felt my cheeks flush and my heart quicken, but I can't say it was an entirely unpleasant sensation.

So Abras is the ears for The Servants. Running the wheelbarrow back and forth and into the collecting area where guards and higher ups congregate allows him to overhear a good deal of valuable information.

Gemi is the portal to the outside. Since she works in the kitchen, she takes in the deliveries from a man who is loyal to The Servants, so we are able to get notes and sometimes even other goods into and out of the mine. That is how Teetee's note got to me.

And Granna, I'm not exactly sure what her role is, but she seems to be at the center of the whole thing, right alongside Onaris. The more I watch those two, the clearer it becomes that their feelings for each other are very strong. They seem to be able to have entire conversations with a nod or laugh or sometimes even a knowing look.

Onaris has to keep out of The Servants for the most part so as not to draw attention. Since he's a known leader, it wouldn't be wise for him to take up his role here in any major way. And Abras told me that on Onaris's first day here, the head guard whipped him in front of the entire slave camp, and only when Onaris was slumped over unconscious, did the guard turn to the onlooking slaves and announce, "Any slave who conspires with this known traitor will meet the same fate."

Of course, it was Granna who tended to his wounds, so bad that Onaris couldn't move for days. Message sent. But despite their gruesome warning, it seems just Onaris's presence brings an infectious energy to the whole operation, and that is as important a contribution as any.

So, while a sixteenth birthday as a slave inside a gold mine may seem bleak, I find myself hoping that there might just be the smallest fuss.

The night of our little celebration arrives. After dinner, we all pull our pallets around in our usual huddle. Granna has woven a little crown out of wild tilla grass, and she places it on my head. I reach up to touch it gently and smile at her.

"Happy birthday, granddaughter." She smiles back. "Gemi was able to get something really special in the last delivery," Granna whispers.

I turn to Gemi, who produces a tiny jar of cruberry jam and six crusts of bread. She spreads a thin layer on each piece and gives us each one. I smile and take a bite, letting the tart sweetness linger on my tongue as long as I can before swallowing. I imagine the others do the same, but I can't be sure because my eyes are closed until I lick the very last morsel from my lips.

Then everyone goes around and tells about their birthday celebrations from their past lives. We laugh and cry until at last we crawl under our blankets to give ourselves over to sleep, the taste of cruberry jam still sweet on our breaths.

I'm in that hazy space between wake and sleep when I hear a gentle voice next to me whisper, "Cala."

I open my eyes to see Abras kneeling next to me. I prop up on my elbow to face him.

"What?" I whisper back.

"Happy Birthday." And he offers his open palm, upon which sits his crust of bread with a smear of cruberry jam. I glance from the bread to his shy smile, and I can't tell which is the greater gift.

"Thank you, Abras," I manage before taking the crust.

I wait until he slips back into the shadows to savor the last bit of my birthday.

***

Three days after my birthday celebration, we're gathered in the camp yard for the morning counting. I'm lost in the warmth of the sunlight on my face when the jolt of a rough hand on my shoulder brings me back to my surroundings.

"Over there," says the gruff voice of a guard, pointing to a small group forming next to a wagon.

I look to Granna, who says, "Go child, you'll be all right." But the worried expression on her face says something else altogether.

So I go, rising panic surging from my belly, when I feel another touch on my shoulder, this time softer. Abras gives me a gentle squeeze as I turn to see his face. His smile reminds me to be brave.

It's not until we are piled into the back of the wagon, our voices drowned out by the rickety wagon wheels and the clip clop of the horse's steps, that we dare to whisper to one another.

"Where are we going?" I ask.

"I don't know," Abras replies. "But it will be okay."

And I believe him.

Soon, we arrive at the base of a wall of gray rock jutting up from the ground. We mill around for a few minutes before another cart pulls up next to us. The guard driving the horse hops down, walks around back, and pulls off the canvas tarp covering the wagon to reveal mounds of coarse black powder.

"Fire powder," Abras whispers. "They're gonna blast open a new mine."

The thought of this sends rage coursing through me. *A new mine! More! Is that what they want? More gold? More bodies? More darkness?* But it isn't really they that floods my mind. It's he. It's my father that I picture as I am overcome with rage.

It isn't long before the process is laid out for us. Abras is brought to be the runner, only this time, he'll be running the fire powder from the wagon into the mines. Soon, I learn what my job will be. After the first blast carves out a gaping hole in the side of the mountain, I'm to crawl into the crevices with a pouch of fire powder tied around my waist. Once I get as far as I can force my body, I'll dump the contents of the pouch out. Then, I'll take a spool of thin rope that they hang around my neck. As I back my way out of the mine, I'll slowly unravel the rope beneath me. Then, they'll light the rope, let it travel the long path back into the mine crevice, and simple as that, they've made a new crevice to swallow me whole.

Everything about this new job is torture. The floor of the freshly exploded crevice is littered with bits of rock that cut into my hands and knees, leaving them bloody and raw by the end of the day. The smell of the fire powder is somehow both metallic and rotten, and I find myself gagging as much as breathing. The crevices are low and narrow, and my back aches with each unnatural movement as I make the long trek in and the long trek back out.

By the end of the day, my body feels like the side of the rock face looks: decimated.

Mercifully, the day has passed, and I find myself back on the wagon next to Abras. He looks at my face, caked in dirt, fire powder, and tears. He lifts his thumb to wipe away the residue on my face.

"There you are," he says with an attempt at a smile.

I begin to smile back, but somehow that even hurts.

When I finally make my way back to our sleeping quarter, Granna takes me in with a frown: back hunched, hands and knees bleeding with a hundred tiny cuts.

"Oh, you poor child," she gasps and sets to work fixing me up. She washes my skin and hair, which takes a good deal of vigorous scrubbing. Producing a salve that she has made with marin root from the camp yard, she rubs it on my hands and knees. Then she rubs my back and my shoulders until I can almost sit upright. She feeds me soup right there on my pallet until I cannot fight my drooping eyelids any longer.

When I wake, every muscle throbs. I lay on my pallet with my eyes closed, imagining which body part I might give up if it meant being back in my old bed with my blue flower blanket pulled over my head.

I'm contemplating my left middle finger when Granna gently shakes me.

"Wake up, child. Any longer, and you'll miss the counting."

That's enough to get me moving. I saw the example they made of the last slave who missed the counting, and it is not a fate I wish to share.

Granna wraps my hands and knees with torn pieces of her spare tunic to keep them from getting bloodied again. She pulls my hair back and ties it into a knot on top of my head. Then she wraps a scarf around my hair.

"Well, that will have to do," she says, handing me a crust of bread as we turn to make our way to the counting.

***

The weeks pass in a blur of fire powder and dirt, but something begins to change. In the dark crevices of the new mine, my wild imaginings start to take a different form. They're no longer the nightmares of Teetee being tortured or Sentaya and Rayon suffering my father's wrath.

Now, in flitted images, I see the gaping wounds on Onaris's back from the warning whipping delivered by the head guard. I see Gemi's delicate hands blistering as the kitchen guard burns them with scalding water. I see Willa's fearful eyes as she is cornered in the shadows of the camp yard, sometimes clawing her way to escape the clutches of the night guard. Sometimes not.

But soon those flitted images are interrupted with others. I see my mother, no older than myself, joining The Servants alongside my grandfather to bring good into this world. I imagine her and Teetee conspiring in the secret of our bedroom to bring down my father and all he stands for. And I imagine Teetee slipping out into the night, knowing the risk that she could and did face, to carry on my mother's dream, to ensure that her sacrifice was made for something. With each imagining, I feel braver and I feel angrier. And I understand that I must take up their work to bring down what is dark in this world, to protect the people I love — and the ones I don't even know — from its brutality. And I will begin with this cursed mine.

And it is then that it dawns on me that I am right in the heart of it all with fire powder in my hands.

***

The Servants in the mine must meet with the utmost caution. The plan is that it cannot appear that there is any plan at all. So, they meet at different intervals of time with different members present each time at different locations. All this is done to ensure that it never appears as if a secret organization is carrying on right in the middle of a slave camp.

When I approach Granna about joining the next meeting, she is hesitant. I gather that this is to protect me as much as it is to protect The Servants.

"It's too risky," she insists. "I admire your spirit, Cala, I really do, but this is beyond your sixteen years."

"I must do this, Granna. I must carry out what they started." I don't have to name my mother and Teetee for her to understand what I aim to do.

"They weren't sixteen-year-old slaves in a mine!" she counters. "And even still, look where it got them."

I close my eyes to gather myself. Without opening them, I press on.

"This anger, Granna, the only way to get it out is to take him down. I'm afraid if I don't it will settle into my heart, and I will lose myself to it."

She considers this for some time before she sighs deeply and says, "When the moon is highest in the sky, make your way to the mouth of the mine."

***

That night, I lie awake as the moon makes its agonizingly slow ascent. I go over the details of my plan. I need them to agree to it. Without The Servants, I'm no more than a sixteen-year-old in a slave mine, as Granna says.

When the moon is finally highest in the sky, I stalk through the shadows to the mouth of the mine. Just inside, there's a little alcove that dips to the right. I follow it until I discover three figures tucked into the corner where the light of their candle isn't visible from the mouth. As I move closer, the candle illuminates three faces: Onaris, Abras, and a third woman whom I've seen but never met.

"Hello there, Cala," Onaris tips his head. "This is Zelaya."

I glance to the woman standing between Abras and Onaris, the dancing flame illuminating her copper skin and speckled brown eyes.

Zelaya takes me in, her tight-lipped expression unchanging. She says nothing by way of greeting. I can see that she will take some winning over.

"Hello," I say meekly. This is not getting off to a good start.

"Pru says you have something you want to bring to us," Onaris urges me on.

I look to Abras, who gives me his warm smile and a slight nod of encouragement. I take a deep breath and begin.

"As you know, my father runs this mine. And as much as I want to bring him down, this is about something much bigger. You all know the stories of the people brought here. The stories of the people born here." I pause to look at Abras. "This shouldn't be anybody's story," I say, starting to feel the conviction behind the words.

"No one here disagrees with that, Cala," Onaris says kindly. "But what would you have us do about it?"

"Blow it out of existence."

I pause to see each of them take this in. Then I tell them my plan.

"Every day, when I go into the new mine, I'll smuggle out a little fire powder in a small pouch that I'll conceal under my tunic. I already tested it out." I produce a small pouch to show them.

Onaris pulls the candle back instinctively, and I tuck the pouch safely away. "Go on," he says.

"Well, I'll smuggle out a little more each day. As long as I leave enough in the crevices to make it blow, they won't know that any's missing. When we have enough, we'll get anyone we can to take a little bit down into the old mine to spread it far into the tunnels and shafts. Then we blow it up. That's the easy part."

"And what's the hard part?" Onaris asks.

"The hard part is getting the people out. If we blow up the mine but the people are still here, they'll just put us to work making the new mine. And we'll still be slaves. Slaves who've made their masters very angry."

"Like kicking a cytha hive," Abras offers with a slight grin.

"Yes, exactly." I fight the urge to grin back and carry on. "That's where The Servants would come in. We'd have to smuggle everyone out, to safe places or their families or anywhere we can arrange. I don't have all that figured out. We'd have to have people on the outside waiting to get everyone away. And we'll need a person on the inside."

"How do you see us managing that?" Zelaya speaks for the first time.

"We need a Servant to get a job as a guard of the mine." I hear Zelaya scoff, but I press on. "The new mine, the one we're blasting, they've built a fence there, but they can't finish it until we're done blasting because the ground is unstable, and the fence wouldn't hold up to the blasts."

"It's true," Abras cuts in. "They guard it heavily when we're there, but at night, who knows?"

"I do. I went there last night."

"What!" Abras exclaims. "How did you get there? It's nearly an hour ride by wagon."

"I ran. Very quickly."

"Cala, that was very dangerous," Onaris chides obligatorily. But I am certain I detect a hint of pride as well.

"True as that may be, it's unguarded. They think it's too far to worry about. So, if we had it all arranged, so The Servants were there waiting for us, we could get people out. The only thing I can't figure out is the fuse. We'd have to have something long enough that burns slow enough to give us time to make our escape."

"Tilla grass," says a voice behind us, and we all spin around to see Granna standing in the shadows. She steps into the light. "My mother dried it and used it as the wick in our candles. It burned slowly and steadily, lasted for hours when one of my mother's patients labored through the night." She gives me a wink.

"Something like this would take months to plan, Cala, maybe years," Onaris says. "We'd have to get one of ours on the inside. We'd have to get placement for all the slaves who wanted to escape. Smuggling out enough fire powder alone, would take that long. And all that time we'd have to keep it a secret, make sure the guards didn't find out somehow, or we'd all see the gallows for sure."

"You're right," I say. "It will take time. And a lot of planning. And no small amount of risk. But if we fail, which we might, we will do so knowing that we didn't just take what they gave us. That we fought for something better. For Gemi to get to see her baby before she's half grown. For Abras to set foot outside these walls for the first time in his life. For Granna not to have to live out her last years in the dark of this cursed mine. I'd rather die fighting for my right to live than live my life half-dead in this mine. And maybe we won't die. Maybe we get to live our lives with the sun on our faces and our arms around people we love."

The words disappear into the darkness, and the silence settles around us.

"I'll fight for that." It's Zelaya who speaks first, and from the looks of the group, I'm not the only one who's surprised by it.

"Me too," says Abras. "I'll fight with you, Cala."

Onaris takes one final steadying breath. "Well, we'll have to take it to the others, but if we can get the consensus, I'd be honored to join you in that fight."

We all turn to Granna. She has tears in her eyes when she says, "You are something to behold, granddaughter." And then she narrows her eyes and lowers her voice and says with the fierceness of a queen, "They cannot possibly imagine what is coming."

Chapter 6
Elina
Arcalia: Twenty-one Years Earlier

As breakfast came to an end, I gathered that I was going to receive no help from my lead. I tried my best to recall Ricard's tour from the night before and made my way to the main training room.

Various small weapons ranging from knives to cleavers to batons were laid out on a table near a large round sparring mat. So it would be hand-to-hand combat training. My lips curled into a self-assured smile. My specialty.

"Elina, I presume?" An old man in a brown robe approached me. His bald head gleamed in the candle light, punctuated with tufts of white hair along the sides and back.

I bowed my head. Despite everything, deference to my trainers was something that had been irrevocably ground into me over the years.

"I am Harthan Smittal," he said. "But to this lot, I am known as Smitts."

"I am honored to meet you," I said with a slight bow of the head.

"The honor is mine." He bowed back.

Slowly, the five junior assassins made their way into the training room, each one with their own brand of contempt and suspicion. I had been temporarily thrust into enough bonded groups over the years to feel quite comfortable in the role of outsider. Most times, I preferred it that way.

Ricard's words about boastfulness echoed in my ears, but certainly a proud posture and condescending smirk were allowed.

"Junior assassins, meet Elina. She is the new apprentice. I expect you to show her the same courtesy you were extended in your early days," Smitts said to the group that had now formed a semicircle around him.

"So, none?" retorted a scrappy looking kid, who couldn't be much older than I was. The hulking sidekick that he walked in with laughed rather oafishly.

"Perhaps courtesy is more easily extended to those who don't irritate the rest of us with tiresome comments," said Smitts.

That wiped the smirk off the face of Scrappy and his sidekick.

"Today will be hand-to-hand combat," Smitts said. "However, the exercise will be adapting to whatever weapon you have at your disposal."

He pulled back a cloth to reveal a second set of objects on the table.

"As you know, when you are on a job, many things can go awry. A superior assassin is prepared to use any object that they can acquire in defense or attack."

He gestured to the objects on the table: a candlestick, a glass goblet, a fireplace poker, a horseshoe, a bit of rope, and a long metal key.

"Thanks to Elina's arrival, we now have an even pairing. We will compete in order of seniority, with each competitor choosing their weapon. Junior Assassin Sarrel and Junior Assassin Yera, you will compete first."

The hulking sidekick — Sarrel, apparently — strode over to the table and selected the fire poker without hesitation. He moved to the sparring mat, smacking the poker into his open palm while he awaited his opponent.

Yera stepped forward. Yera was the only assassin who came in alone at the beginning of the training session. Her petite figure seemed miniature next to Sarrel, but I had the distinct sense she was not to be underestimated. Her long black braid swooshed slightly behind her as she made her way to the table. She picked up each of the remaining weapons and considered each one carefully. Eventually she settled on the glass goblet, which she swiftly broke against the table leg before holding it in front of her like a shank and baring her teeth slightly as she took to the sparring mat. Not to be underestimated indeed.

"Combat continues until one opponent forces the other off the sparring mat or subdues the other with a fatal maneuver. I needn't remind you that you may not actually carry out the maneuver." Smitts's stern look seemed to linger on Yera for an extra moment or two. I sensed I may be in for a show.

"Junior assassins, are you ready?"

"Ready," they said simultaneously. But while Sarrel's face registered smug confidence, Yera's said something much different, something that could only be described as calculated anger.

"Commence," Smitts directed and the opponents immediately sprang into action.

Using the length of his weapon to his advantage, Sarrel began swinging the fire poker in large arcs in front of him, and with each step forward, he closed the gap between himself and Yera, who was perched at the edge of the mat, waiting for him. The poker seemed a mere twig in his strong arms, and he wielded it with such force that I feared he might thrust Yera off the mat like a flower from its stem.

But with one more step to go until his swinging poker would make contact, Yera leapt into the air above the poker, and landing precisely on its edge, forced it down to the ground with her feet. For a single beat, she was standing on the tip of it, weighing it down so that Sarrel could not continue swinging. Instead, he found himself off kilter from the force of her landing.

In the next swift movement, she crouched down then flew into the air, goblet shank plunged forward toward Sarrel, tackling him to the ground with her momentum. They landed with Yera straddled atop Sarrel, holding the jagged tip of the goblet to Sarrel's throat so that blood began to trickle down his neck.

"Get off of me, you witch," snarled Sarrel.

Yera sat atop Sarrel for a moment longer. She brought her hand to her mouth and licked Sarrel's blood off her thumb.

"I can taste your fear."

With that she leapt to her feet in one motion, dropped the goblet shank on the floor, and walked out of the training hall.

Sarrel retreated to the back of the training hall, glowering and licking his wounds. Well, not literally, of course. That had already been done for him.

I had never seen anything like Yera before. While I had seen speed and nimbleness used as an advantage against a larger, stronger opponent, Yera was something else altogether. Her movements were what I could only describe as feline. This was someone who I might actually learn from.

I watched as the next competitors — Garle, a largely forgettable older teen save for his shock of red hair, and Patra, a fit, young man who seemed to have a permanent smile on his face — approached the weapons table.

"Junior Assassin Patra, you may select first," said Smitts.

Patra selected the candlestick and then Garle the key, predictably. They were an even match, so we watched for some time as they circled each other, weapons out, in a series of advances and evasions. They were quick and skilled, but neither had a particularly noteworthy fighting style, and I lost interest quickly. Eventually, Garle forced Patra backward off the mat, releasing us from tedium.

I was up. Now, we would see what Scrappy could do.

"Junior Assassin, Felux, you may select first."

Scrappy — Felux — chose the rope. So he wasn't a total fool.

"Apprentice Elina, the horseshoe is yours."

I took the horseshoe and weighed the iron in my hands. This would do just fine.

"Junior Assassin, apprentice, are you ready?"

I smirked at Felux and nodded. Was that a flicker of fear I detected in his eye? It should be.

"Commence."

Felux did what I would do if I had gotten the rope: he held it taunt and tried to use it to sweep me off my feet. From there, I imagined he'd try to get behind me in a stranglehold.

But I knew it was coming, and I leapt to avoid the rope taking out my legs while simultaneously reaching behind me with the horseshoe. Before he could even register his failed maneuver, I wielded the horseshoe like a hook and plucked the taunt rope from his grip.

Now, I had both weapons. Felux's look of dumbfoundedment was one I have called to my imagination many times since when I needed a good laugh.

He leapt after me, but I dodged him easily. He was angry, and his movements were imprecise. As I dodged, I began to make quick work of tying the horseshoe to the end of the rope.

I sprung back to the opposite side of the sparring mat and began swinging the rope so that the horseshoe made wide arcs in front of me. The heavy iron made a satisfying 'whoop whoop' sound as I swung it. I approached Felux steadily, and he had no choice but to backtrack. Soon, he was on the edge of the mat, with his arms up and his body curved away from me to delay the inevitable. On the last whip around, the horseshoe grazed his tunic, putting a slight tear in it. He teetered back off the mat and glared at me. I smirked back.

Yera had returned and was leaning against the door with her arms crossed, watching. She gave me a slight nod before turning to go.

"Assassins, you are free to train as you wish for the remainder of morning exercises," said Smitts to the group. Then, he walked over to me. "Well played, Apprentice Elina."

"Thank you, Smitts." Outwardly, I accepted his praise with a small smile and humble nod. Inwardly, my chest swelled from the so-longed-for validation. "If I may ask, where does Yera go to train?"

"Yera prefers to train out of doors," he explained. "You are welcome to use any equipment in our training facility to further your skills. I think you will find it is well equipped."

He turned and his robes swayed behind him as he approached another apprentice. I spent the morning training with various weapons and wondering what Yera's outdoor training regime was like.

I was engrossed in throwing knives at a target when a bell chimed and the others began to put away their weapons and make their way to the door.

"You are dismissed, Apprentice Elina," Smitts called gently. "It is time for lunch."

***

"How was training?" asked Ricard as we moved through the lunch line.

"Depends who you ask," I said, nodding over to Sarrel and Felux, who glowered at me from their spot at the table.

"Making friends on the first day, I see," Ricard said laughing.

"Few can resist my charm," I joked back.

"Speaking of charm, will you be dining with Trina again?"

"Tempting, but no. I was hoping to sit with Yera, but I don't see her."

"You won't find her in here," he said. "She takes her meals outside. She's usually in the gardens behind the manor. If you wander back there for a while, you can probably find her."

"It's freezing out!"

He shrugged. "Doesn't seem to bother her. She really only comes in when she has to."

"Huh. Well, hopefully my soup won't freeze by the time I find her."

And with that, I was off in hope that, despite the cold weather, Yera would offer a slightly less frosty reception than Trina.

***

Yera sat on a bench with a red, yellow, and purple woven blanket drawn around her entire body.

"Are you lost?" asked Yera, looking up from her meal. So much for less frosty.

"No, actually. I was hoping I might eat with you."

"Why?"

"I don't know. I've just never seen anyone move like that today. I guess I just wanted to know how you learned to do that."

"You've got a few moves of your own," she offered, warming slightly.

"Thanks. But you were something else entirely. It was like watching an animal move."

She grinned a bit at that. "Well, it should be. That's who I learned from."

"You learned to fight from an animal?"

"Yes."

"What… how did you get an animal to teach you to fight?"

She laughed aloud at that. "I learned through observation. Sit if you're interested. I will tell you."

I sat obediently next to Yera on the bench and did my best not to shiver as I ate my cold soup.

"Mine are the mountain people from the Tunic Mountains. We raise our young with what we call tanouli, which is a sort of deep connection with nature. It goes beyond that. Your people don't have any word that means the same."

"My people?"

"The subjects of Arcalia."

"Aren't you, I mean, aren't the Tunic Mountains in Arcalia?"

"Our mountains are on the land that was long ago declared for Arcalia. But our mountains belong to no one, and neither do we."

I had never in my life considered that one could be anything but a subject of their kingdom—to simply declare that they are bound to no one.

"For us, tanouli is to connect with nature deep within your soul. It is to understand the suffering of a dying tree, to feel the magic of a dancing wind, or to learn the movements of your kimbasa, your kindred animal."

"Kindred animal?"

"We believe each child is born with a kindred animal, a likeness — both in body and in mind — to a certain animal. That child must discover their kimbasa and then learn to harness the energy of their animal through many years of study."

"And your kimbasa?"

"My kimbasa is a neru, which is a mountain cat. I grew very close to my kimbasa, and there was even one that let me run with her for a short time. I hunted and slept and tousled right alongside her."

"Incredible. But how is that even possible?"

"The kimbasa is a two-way connection. Some are gifted with a very strong connection to their kindred animal, as I was. It took many years, but eventually, the neru felt the deep connection and trusted me to join her."

"Is that why... is that why Sarrel called you a witch?"

"Many believe that my people have magical powers that allow us to connect with animals. But it is not magic. The ability to connect your soul to nature is one that we all have, if only we care enough to develop it. It is like a tiny seed inside each of us, but for most, it withers without them ever knowing it was there."

"What would my kimbasa have been?" I wondered aloud.

"What do you think?"

"I would like to think a dirawolf, but sometimes I am afraid I am more of an anterlope," I admitted.

"Why does that make you afraid?"

"An anterlope is weak. It dashes off at the slightest sound."

"Or perhaps an anterlope is wise and knows that there is more to life than killing."

"You sound like Auntie Cook. She serves as much advice as she does food."

We both laughed at that.

"And anyway, if there is more to life than killing, how is it that you find yourself in The Assassins' Guild?" I asked, hoping I hadn't pushed too far.

Yera paused, and I detected a note of sadness as she stared in the opposite direction. Without turning back toward me, she began again. "When I was fourteen, men from your kingdom came to our mountain and said that they were taking back what was rightfully Arcalia's land so that it could be used for farming. Before we understood what was happening, they lit our village and the surrounding forest on fire."

"Oh, Yera. I'm so sorry. Were your people hurt?"

"Did they die? No. But we feel the suffering of nature as if it were our own. So to watch our beloved forest burn, to know that many of our kimbasa were in it, it was a suffering worse than death."

I didn't have any words for that, so we sat in silence for some time.

"My people relocated to another part of the mountain and began to build again. But for me, the anger was too great. It was as if my very heart pulsed anger through my body, burning my skin and pounding in my ears. My only thought was revenge, so eventually I found my way here, where at least I could spend my days killing the people of Arcalia."

"But those people didn't burn your land."

"No? They are all the same to me. And with each life that I take, I cut off another line, and maybe with it, another unborn cruelty that my people will not have to suffer."

"I am so sorry that your people have suffered. But you must understand, there are many good people in Arcalia. Most of us are just trying to make a life for ourselves. And we have suffered at the hand of the king, too."

I'm not sure why I feel the need to defend the Arcalians. Even my parents were by no means innocent. But somehow, I needed Yera to understand, that we weren't all like that. That I wasn't like that.

"Well, let's hope the good people of Arcalia don't end up as any of my marks."

I stared at her a bit incredulously, despite myself.

"Elina, most of the marks that I am contracted to kill are bloated old rich men, who are somehow denying other bloated old rich men from getting what they want."

"But don't those bloated rich men support the king? He isn't concerned with the Assassins' Guild picking off his loyal subjects?"

"He just looks the other way. For a hefty cut of the profit. Everybody has a price, Elina."

She takes in my face, which must register my disillusionment.

"Trust me, Elina, corrupt king or not, the world is better off without these pigs in it."

"I suppose you're right. I guess it just feels like an endless cycle of suffering."

To her credit, she seemed to ponder this for a moment before leaping, cat-like, to her feet. "Well, I'd better get on with my day. Master Sera doesn't tolerate idleness."

And with that, she was gone, leaving me alone in the cold, empty garden to consider whether having an anterlope as my kimbasa would be so terrible a fate.

***

"Where've you been?"

I whipped around in the hallway on the way back to the dining room, my empty bowl still in hand, to see Trina approaching.

"I have my quota meeting, and she wants you present. Further punishment. Let's go."

I fumbled awkwardly with the dish in my hand.

"Just leave it there! Let's go!"

I placed the dish on a windowsill, which seemed disrespectful, especially when you consider that I was the dishwasher. But I was not about to argue with Trina.

Master Sera was waiting for us behind her desk, much the way she was when I met her last night, and while it was hard to tell, her look of contempt seemed to have deepened since I last saw her.

"Elina, I trust Trina is helping you get settled in?"

Trina casted a sideways glance in my direction, which was warning enough for me.

"Oh, yes. Absolutely."

Whether or not Master Sera could detect my insincerity, she turned her attention back to Trina.

"You were one kill short of your quota this month, Trina," Master Sera stated, her words laced with disdain.

"My planning was flawless. The mark had a last-minute change of plan, which put him beyond my reach. He must have been tipped. It was out of my control."

"An assassin does not make mistakes, and she certainly does not make excuses. You lost the guild one of our most lucrative clients."

"I understand, Master Sera," Trina said, her eyes cast down toward the desk.

"You will be demoted to junior assassin until you can once again prove yourself worthy."

I could tell the news was more than Trina expected. She glanced up from the desk and looked at Master Sera with wide eyes and open mouth.

"Most fortuitously, you have an opportunity to prove yourself sitting right here." She gestured toward me — the opportunity apparently.

Master Sera went on. "Elina comes to us as a very promising apprentice. Train her well and see that she passes her final test, and you may earn back your former status."

With that, she rose from her chair behind the desk. "The contract is the only creed."

I found myself rising alongside Trina and answering back, "The mark is the only mission."

We saw ourselves out.

"Do you, uh, want to talk about what happened in there?" I asked as we stood outside Master Sera's office.

Trina huffed and turned on her heel, stomping away, but not before I caught sight of the tears brimming in her eyes.

I gathered that our session was over for today, which gave me time to collapse onto my bed until it was time to help in the kitchen.

***

The highlight of my days quickly became taking lunch outside with Yera. I learned to dress for the cold and listen more than I spoke. Our brief time together was far more of an education than Trina could offer. Although, Yera didn't hide the fact that she was growing tired of taking orders, and it was clear she was becoming restless here.

As for Trina, she was eager as ever to please Master Sera. Soon, she began to plan for her next job, so I got to learn, at least through observation, the way the process worked.

The assassin was assigned a contract that simply had the name of the mark, the location, and the deadline for the kill. From there, the assassin got busy trailing the mark, learning his habits to craft her plan. As I had learned from Trina's exchange with Master Sera, failure was not an option. The assassins had to be meticulous in their planning, but they also had to be efficient because each assassin had to meet a quota of three kills a month. It was far more laborious than I had imagined.

The mark that Trina was preparing for was, in fact, a bloated old rich man who had some dispute over land with his neighbor. Apparently, their estates backed up to a forest the neighbor liked to hunt in, but legally, the land belonged to the mark. So, he went from neighbor to foe, and now Trina would kill him.

It all seemed so terribly unimportant, making it hard to feel any dignity in taking part in such a petty dispute with two men acting like children.

One afternoon, when Trina seemed slightly less closed off than usual, I dared to broach the topic.

"How do you feel about all this?" I asked her.

"I don't."

"You feel nothing for this man that you are about to kill?"

"Nope."

"How can you feel nothing?"

She stopped sharpening her blade for a moment and turned to me. Eye contact was rare for Trina, so I stiffened with attention.

"In this world, you are either the one bringing the pain or receiving it. I've been at the receiving end enough in my life."

"But why does there have to be pain at all?"

"It's just the way of the world, Elina. People are either cruel or weak. Do you think the mark — this landowner who won't give up his forest — do you think he sits on his enormous estate with his eleven wives being kind to people? No. Trust me, killing him will mean a little less cruelty in the world. And it will put a few coins in my pocket."

She went back to sharpening her knife.

"And besides, it's my job not to care. 'The contract is the only creed; the mark is the only mission.' Did you think that was just something nice we say? It's what you're signing on for, Elina. Your feelings have no place here."

I was suddenly hit with the force of something my mother had said when I was a child. "Your emotions are none of my concern." It was when I was just seven or eight years old and scared to leave for another training season.

The words seemed to dig at some old wound, and suddenly I felt my throat constrict and my eyes water. I needed to get away from there.

"Oh, I suddenly remembered that Auntie Cook asked me to come down early to help with dinner."

"Fine. Just finish the log of the guards' shifts tonight."

I dashed out, hoping Trina wouldn't notice that I already had tears streaming down my face.

I wasn't sure where to go. The thought of being alone in my room felt unbearable. Even though I had lied about Auntie Cook needing me early, the mention of her left a lingering warmth, so I found myself heading toward the kitchen anyway.

"What are you doing here? Your shift's not for a few hours yet." Auntie Cook called to me, her focus remaining on the dough she was kneading.

"I just thought I'd come down and see if you needed help."

That got her attention. "Fiddle figs," she said, glancing in my direction. "I know fiction when I hear it."

"I just, I don't know. I needed to be somewhere with someone who would not tell me to stop feeling things." I was crying in earnest now, and I could only imagine how ridiculous I must have sounded.

"Who's telling you to stop feeling things?"

"My mother. Trina. The whole damned world."

"And you're going to listen? That doesn't sound like you."

"What choice do I have? Nobody cared about my feelings then. And it's my job not to feel now. I might as well just be a weapon with no soul for all the world cares."

I slumped into a stool by the kitchen counter, dropped my head into my arms, and let out loud, heaving sobs.

"Well, you don't seem to be having any trouble feeling things from where I'm standing."

Then I was laugh-sobbing. "I don't know how to stop feeling!"

"Of course you don't. You're a person, not a weapon. You don't think Trina feels things? Not feeling things and not admitting that you feel things are two entirely different matters."

I considered that.

"Believe me when I tell you, Elina. There isn't a person in this world who doesn't feel things. You have to learn to be okay with your feelings, whatever they are. Honor them even. Feelings are your heart's way of giving you advice."

"Where do you come up with this stuff?"

"A lot of hours alone in this kitchen, talking to bread."

I laughed.

"See? There you go. Another feeling. Good for you!"

"And what advice is my heart trying to give me now?"

"Your heart is saying that since you found your way down to the kitchen, you may as well stay to help. Here's an apron."

I spent the rest of that evening in the warmth of the kitchen with Auntie Cook, feeling all my feelings and thinking that my heart had given me very good advice indeed.

***

As the night of the kill approached, Trina developed a plan to take advantage of the front gate guard's shift change to slip into the estate. The door to the servants' quarters didn't latch properly, so she would sneak into the house through there then make her way up two floors and into the master sleeping quarters. Apparently, the man preferred to sleep alone, so once he was done with one of his wives for the night, he would send her back to her quarters.

Trina had made it very clear that she did not want me to come along, but she grudgingly agreed, solely out of self-interest to earn back her position. I was to follow behind her, nothing more than a shadow, observing her methods.

I approached the night with a strange combination of excitement and dread. It was what I was here for. And after our meticulous planning, I was ready to finally put the plan into action.

But I simultaneously dreaded it as I had never seen someone killed, and I wasn't sure how it would feel. During my stint with the slave trader, there was a young man who took a blow to the head during a fight and became unresponsive. The slave trader carted him off to a doctor, but he never returned. For months, I was tormented by the image of the man as I tried to fall asleep, his face looking almost peaceful save the sticky blood matting his hair. In my seven-year-old mind, it was an accident, not a senseless cruelty endured by one who had not chosen to fight at all.

But this was no slave. Just a haughty, loathsome man who had made himself a target with his own pettiness. Surely, he deserved what was coming for him.

***

I shadowed Trina as she snuck onto the estate—past the guards as they changed shifts, and through the door of the servants' quarter that didn't quite latch. Every sense was awakened, and my body was alive with the thrill of it.

Inside the manor, we slunk against the walls, even though the house was pitch back and silent at that hour. We made our way up two flights of stairs and through the hallway until we were at the master's quarters. Trina unlatched the door silently and we slipped inside.

We approached the bed, guided by the steady snore of the mark. A strip of moonlight cascaded across his legs, and I saw them shift slightly under his blanket.

The thrill dissolved instantly. He was alive, snoring and shifting his legs. To know that life coursed through him, and soon it would not, suddenly became unbearable. I was overcome with an urgency to wrest the knife from Trina's grip, to yell out, to do anything to save this man's life. But I remained a shadow on the wall.

Within moments the snoring gave way to gurgling as Trina slit his throat. In the moonlight, his legs thrashed in panic. I bore witness to the gurgling and thrashing for some time longer before all went quiet and still.

The silence that followed crept into my soul and settled in. I never even saw his face.

Somehow, I made it until we were off the estate before I vomited.

***

The following afternoon, when Trina received her next contract, she was cheerful. Well, cheerful for Trina. Her first successful kill for the month meant she was on track to meet her quota.

She read the information on the contract and apparently knew the location well, prattling on about the potential approaches.

But all I could hear was the gurgling of the man's slit throat. I wanted to scream to drown out the noise.

"Elina, are you even listening to me?"

"Yes," I said, attention returning.

"Elina, you're going to have to manage. You can't let every kill get to you like this. It's just a job."

"I'm not. I won't. I'm fine. Go on."

I glanced up, and unexpectedly, I found her eyes cast down in a look of, what, shame?

"Elina, listen. She makes me report everything. So I had to tell her how you... handled things."

"How I handled things?"

"You know. The vomiting and then sobbing all the way back afterward."

"Oh, I didn't know you could hear that."

"Yeah."

"Okay, so what, I'm out?"

"No, you're not out. But she has her ways."

"What does that mean?"

"She spreads the information, so all the assassins know."

"What? Everyone knows?"

"If not already, soon. And there's more."

"What more?"

"She has them call you 'worm' until you shadow me and don't... do that."

"Worm?"

"Yeah, spineless."

The devastation and shock of her news must have registered on my face.

"It's just the way of things. The next kill isn't too far off. Just try to keep it together next time."

It was as close to words of encouragement as I'd gotten so far from my lead.

***

As I walked into the dining hall at dinner, the room went silent.

Suddenly, the assassins up and down the length of the table began to yell out, "Worm!" Some, like Felux and Sarrel, jeered with great satisfaction. Others, like Ricard and Trina, called out more half-heartedly. But every one of them joined the shaming chorus of, "Worm".

It took a great force of will not to run sobbing out of the dining hall.

My eyes watered as I dazedly served food onto my plate, but I held the tears back. I was desperate to be able to hold the feelings back as well. I had come here to be an assassin because I had yearned to kill before. And now, I was sickened at the thought of killing and being shamed for it.

Perhaps I would simply need to train the compassion out of me — beat it out if need be. Focus.

The contract is the only creed. The mark is the only mission. There was no room for emotion here.

"Here love, have some tea." Auntie Cook offered a mug as I came down to the kitchen after dinner. "You looked beside yourself this morning."

All I wanted to do was take the warm mug and cry to Auntie Cook. To give voice to my rising doubt.

But instead, I silenced it.

"I'm fine," I said, brushing past her toward the dishes.

"Ah, I see then," she said as she put the mug on top of the pile of dirty dishes and went back to her work.

When I caught a glimpse of her face as she passed by, I braced myself for the anger. But it wasn't anger I found in Auntie Cook's eyes. It was disappointment.

Chapter 7
Cala
Urendia

"It's been almost a year! The time is now!" I exclaim in an urgent whisper. A small group of The Servants are huddled together in the back corner of the kitchens. "We are almost done with the new mine. Soon, they'll close the fence."

"I understand, Cala. But the guards have gotten word that something is being planned. They are on high alert. It's too risky right now," reasons Haviel, our inside man. After a timely accident that left one of the guards without the use of his right leg, Haviel managed to get himself hired as the replacement. On nights that he has overnight watch, we are able to hold a meeting in the kitchens with little risk of being discovered.

"The fire powder is spread among the slaves," I shoot back. "The tilla grass is dried and ready. We just need to give the signal, and it's done!"

"You're forgetting that we don't have all the placements yet," says Willa. "The note Gemi got just yesterday said they're still waiting to secure dozens of locations for the slaves. Haviel's right, Cala."

I look to Abras for support, but he isn't looking at me. I press on.

"We can find the last of the placements once we get everyone out. Surely we can find people to take them in."

"You're living in a fairy tale," Zelaya hisses. "People don't just take in slaves off the street. And the guards suspect something. I want out of this place as much as you do, Cala, as much as anybody does, but now is not the right time."

"We'll figure out the fence, Cala. We'll find a way," Willa tries to reassure. Haviel nods. Abras still looks away.

If I stay here a second longer, I'll explode. I'll take it out on these people, my people, who have risked everything for this plan.

So I turn with a huff and storm outside. I'm behind the mess hall, letting my rage simmer into the cool night air when I hear Abras approach. I wait for him to comfort me. Except he doesn't.

"How can you be so childish?"

His anger is a flash of lightning from a clear blue sky, and it sends me reeling.

"What? I—"

"You've been here a year, Cala, a year! I've been here my whole life!"

"I know, Abras, but I—"

"And we're so close to making this impossible thing actually happen, and you can't just wait a little longer."

"Okay, I will. I'm sorry."

His face softens now, and his shoulders relax, a clear blue sky once again. He continues, but more gently now.

"This is bigger than you now, Cala. There are a lot of people who didn't let themselves imagine another story. But they have now because of what you've done. They've imagined their stories, and there's no taking that back from them now."

I thought about that. The many people in this mine, imagining their stories, their lives outside this dark place. And I understand the responsibility of it. I turn toward him. "You're right," I say. "And what about you, Abras? What story do you imagine?"

He looks at me then, for the first time since he's come outside. He takes my two hands in his and he pulls me closer to him.

"You, Cala. You're my story."

He pulls me closer still. And then there is no space between us at all, and Abras's arms are around my waist, and mine are around his neck. The soft brush of his lips against mine take me somewhere else, and for this small moment in time, we aren't here at all. We are living our story.

***

Word from Teetee has been sporadic, but enough has come through to understand what has happened to her. Despite whatever they've put her through, which I try not to think about, Teetee must not have revealed anything about The Servants because the only crimes they accuse her of in the end are 'Learning to Write' and 'Teaching a Girl to Write'. She is sentenced to ten years' hard labor. Of course, my father wouldn't put her in the gold mine, knowing that our being together would be too much of a gift, so she's sent to the camps in the countryside, where prisoners can be put to work by farmers, free of charge.

When I first learn of the news, I express relief that she can be outside and not in the dark mine, but Granna explains that life in the fields can be just as cruel as life in the mines.

"Some farmers are kinder than others, but the slaves toil in the heat from sun up until sun down, picking the prula seed from its prickly stalk or crawling on their hands and knees to dig out caters from the ground. They're fed and housed at the mercy of the farmer, and some see it as their right to treat them like animals, worse than."

"I hope Teetee got placed with a kind farmer," I say. This thought becomes a prayer I find myself uttering often.

"Me too, child," says Granna.

Getting Teetee free has been a part of the plan. We haven't gotten word from The Servants on the outside, and the uncertainty of it plagues me. Another part of the plan is to get Rayon and Sentaya out, if they choose to, which I desperately hope they will.

Granna, and me, and our people in the mine, plus my people out of the mine, will travel together to Arcalia, back to Granna's home. We've gotten word that the farm still seems to be in Granna's family, but the details aren't quite clear. So, we'll travel as a group to the neighboring kingdom and make our way to Granna's farm, hopeful that we'll receive a warm welcome from her kin.

That will be our story.

When Abras and I are in the cart on the way to the new mine one morning, our voices drowned out by the rickety wheel and the clip clop of the horse, we imagine our story on Granna's farm.

"I don't care about the rest," Abras says. "But there must be a sheep named Elanora."

I laugh. Sitting here with our arms touching and sun warming our faces, our story begins to feel less and less like a dream.

But as we approach the mine, we spot two unusual things: a crew already at work and a torch. As we get closer we can see that they are using a flame to weld the last piece of the iron fence — along with our escape plan — shut.

***

It is four days until Haviel has overnight watch. So for those four, long days before we can meet again in the back of the kitchens, The Servants in the mine hang their heads a bit lower than usual. If you weren't looking for it, they would simply be downcast slaves, dejected about their lot in life. But I see it for what it is: the brokenness that comes when someone dares to imagine a better story, only to have to have it fade like a warm dream at dawn.

When we finally gather, desperation is heavy as we try to find a way around that iron wall.

"We could dig a tunnel under it," Gemi offers. "At night, a few at a time. We could run there the way Cala did."

"With what tools?" questions Zeyana.

"And even if we could find the tools, how would we hide the dug hole and dirt from the guards during the day?" Abras adds.

"We could drug the guards," I suggest. "Use Granna's lock weed."

"And then what?" says Zeyana. "March all eighty-seven slaves out the front gates? Into the streets without anybody noticing or alerting the authorities?"

The room becomes quiet, and desperation starts to give way to hopelessness.

After some time, Zeyana breaks the silence. "My people have a story."

Zenaya has our attention as she has never spoken about her homeland.

"There once was a serpent who trapped a herd of zebreyas in an enclosure. The walls were thick with bramble vines, and any zebreya who tried to leap over to escape would get caught. The serpent would leave the caught zebreya, bloodied from the bramble thorns, as an example for the others. Before long, no zebreyas tried to escape.

"The serpent would slither through the forest, boasting, 'I have trapped a herd of zebreyas. Their stripes are white as snow and black as night. They are mine to gaze at whenever I please.'

"One day, a clever zebreya overheard the serpent boasting to the jaguire, and he understood that the serpent was weakened by his pride.

"He said to the serpent, 'The animals of the forest cannot know the treasure you have won yourself if they cannot see it. They likely do not believe that you are as great as you say. For you know the saying goes, 'It is with one's ears that they hear but only with their eyes that they truly believe.'

"The serpent scoffed, but the idea began to fester. Surely the animals would know his greatness if they could see his treasure for themselves. But the bramble vine was too thick, and only the serpent could slither in and out through the small gaps.

"I will open up the wall just slightly so that the jaguire can see inside, the serpent thought. Then he will know the beauty of my treasure, and he will tell the rest of the forest animals.

"But the clever zebreya had told the herd, and they were ready. When the serpent opened the bramble weed to show the jaguire, they charged the opening and forced their way past the jaguire and the serpent, springing away in every direction."

The final words of Zelaya's story hang in the air as we picture the beautiful herd of striped zebreyas springing into the forest.

"The wall is closed. We will not escape by luck, and we cannot escape by force. But we can escape by trickery," she says with an impish grin on her face.

I can feel the hopelessness beginning to dissipate.

"The serpent was weakened by his pride, but it is something else that weakens the powerful men of these mines."

"Greed," offers Abras.

"Precisely," Zeyana replies. "And who is the greediest of them all?" she asks, looking at me now.

"My father," I say, contempt lacing my voice.

"Yes, your father. So we will use his weakness against him. We will be the trickster zebreya. And he will open the door to let us out."

***

There is a lord who lives on the outskirts of the kingdom in an estate nestled into the Gralestone Hills.

The particulars of this lord's life are not important. In fact, he himself doesn't enter our plan at all. What is important is that — thanks to a recently plundered carriage — The Servants have come to possess an exact replica of his seal. They have not yet had occasion to use it. For once they use the seal, and the artifice is eventually discovered, the seal will no longer be useful. They have been saving it for a worthy scheme, a scheme such as ours.

Time is in our favor, but it will not be for long. Haviel has told us that, in the coming weeks, there will be a brief window of time when the equipment from the old mine must be moved to the new mine. It will take some time to break down the equipment inside the mine, haul it out, transport it to the new mine, haul it in, and assemble it for use. The planners of the new mine predict that this operation will take roughly two weeks, and according to Haviel's information, my father is furious at the wasted days of mining. Despite his wrath and several replaced planners, there doesn't seem to be any way around the two-week delay.

At the height of my father's rage, he receives a letter.

To the Overseer of the Urendia Gold Mine,

I write to you, one businessman to another, with a proposition. I have recently discovered a deposit of silver in the hills on my land. I have already arranged a deal with an Arcalian trader, who is anxiously waiting for the supply. I have been able to assemble the equipment, but I don't have the labor.

I understand that you run an efficient mine, so it seems an opportunity has arisen that might benefit us both. If you can supply the labor, I will offer you half of the profit in exchange.

If you find this arrangement agreeable, I will send wagons to collect the slaves in two weeks' time. My associate will arrange the details.

Signed,

Lord Claremont of the Gralestone Hills.

My father rereads the letter and then checks the broken seal.

A prudent man might respond with skepticism, perhaps take several measures to confirm the authenticity of such an improbably fortuitous offer beyond merely glancing at a broken seal.

But like the serpent with his pride, my father is weakened by his greed, so when Lord Claremont's associate arrives at my father's house a few days later, he welcomes him in and calls to his wives to prepare a meal.

"Your timing couldn't be better," he says with a smug grin. "Please, please, come in."

And so, a man by the name of Brayan, who, as it turns out, has never met Lord Claremont, mirrors my father's grin and steps inside.

***

During my time in the mine, I have resisted the urge to send word to my siblings so as not to endanger them through any connection to The Servants. But the days are few and the lives at stake are many, and so, it is time to contact Sentaya and Rayon.

It is too risky to send written word lest it be intercepted, so Brayan, who has continued to visit my father's house as they plan, has sent information that Sentaya now helps with the market shopping. There's a Servant in the city who has a cousin with a vegetable stall in the market, so on this market day, the Servant has taken over the stall, waiting to intercept Sentaya.

She will wrap the vegetables in a square of canvas that Sentaya will hang on the outside of the gate at my father's house. Sentaya will try to overhear my father's work as best she can — serving tea or clearing dishes when he meets with his associates — and if she gets any sense that he has discovered our plan, she will draw an X on the canvas to give the signal to abandon our mission.

The other message is that she and Rayon have a place in our wagon. Should they decide to leave, they are to wait for us at the fountain on the eastern edge of the city an hour after sunrise on the morning of The Traveling.

The Traveling is how the guards referred to it when they instructed us on the plan to load us into wagons and travel to the Gralestone Hills to work Lord Claremont's mines. So we've adopted their name to avoid suspicion but also because it described our plan as well.

Except that we won't travel to the Gralestone Hills. The eighty-seven slaves of this mine will be loaded into the nine wagons, headed for nine different destinations. The Servants on the outside have been busy securing safe locations into the far reaches of the kingdom and beyond. Using the records smuggled out by Haviel, they have arranged for safe destinations for every soul enslaved in this mine. The enormity of their efforts brings me to tears every time I think about it. Not just The Servants spread across the kingdom, using every connection and calling in every favor, but the kind citizens of Urendia. They have opened their homes or their barns or their workshops — whatever safe space they could offer — for small groups of strangers to land as they determine their next moves. It would be impossible to deliver the slaves to their families, at least not at first, as that is the first place the guards would look.

Of course, most of the eighty-seven are not aware of any of this. To them, The Traveling is just another order for their tired bodies to carry out. A plan this precious, this intricate, would not be secure beyond the small group of trusted Servants, and so we had to make the choice for them. To leave them behind, especially knowing the cruelty that would await them once we kicked the cytha hive as Abras put it, would make us no better than my father. So, we made the choice for them, hoping that any sort of story, however fraught and uncertain it may be, would be better than no story at all.

Of the many steps of the plan I have played and replayed in my mind, I often find myself imagining the moment when my father learns the news. To watch his face flush red and his fists curl with impotent rage the precise second he understands that his cargo did not arrive at its destination, it's almost enough to tempt me to stay behind. Almost.

But no. I will be among the eighty-seven slaves, slaves no longer — plus Rayon and Sentaya if all goes accordingly — when one by one the wagons peel away from the train like so many seeds carried off by the wind.

So, it is on this market morning a Servant waits at her cousin's vegetable stall, scanning the crowd. And I find myself imagining a very different face: Sentaya's wild green eyes, widening with surprise, followed instantly by her mouth twisting into her toothy grin as the vegetable peddler calls out to her.

"I have word from the Kingdom of Cressida."

***

In the final days before The Traveling, all communication with The Servants on the outside has stopped. Barring some major news or catastrophe, it was decided that it was safest not to arouse any unnecessary suspicion as the day approached. After furious scheming for the better part of a year, these final days feel suddenly vacant. But quickly our varied emotions, largely suppressed these last months in the midst of the planning, begin to fill the vacant space. We feel hope, of course, hope that our stories which have come to seem so real in our imaginings, might truly become real. That we might smell our homelands and hold our loved ones and breathe clean air into our sooty lungs.

And fear, fear that it could all go wrong. There are a hundred details that could go wrong, and any one of them would doom not only us, but the other slaves whose choice we have made. Late at night, as the darkness tightens around me, the fear grips me, giving way to panic and terror, and it seems impossible that it will go our way.

In those moments, I lean on the others to steady me. Granna soothes, "Hush, child. Have hope."

Or Abras jokes, "If we don't make it, who will feed Elanora?" And then I find hope again, and I carry on.

And somehow, sadness pierces through it all, a strange emotion to be feeling on the eve of our freedom, and yet, there it is. The Traveling means that some of us will say goodbye to one another. Gemi, of course, will go to her daughter. But as heavy as my heart is at saying goodbye to my friend, it is equally light with the thought of her holding her daughter in her arms, getting to see some of her childhood, kissing her cheeks while they are still round and soft.

Zeyana's wagon will head south to her homeland, or at least as far south as it can take her before she will have to find her own way. Sometimes I see her staring into empty space, her lips curved up into the smallest trace of a smile, and I wonder if she is imagining her home, her unfinished story that she will return to. Beyond the tale of the serpent and the zebreya, Zeyana has never shared anything about her homeland. Perhaps, after being forced from your home and enslaved across the sea, your story is all that is yours, and it becomes much too precious a gift to share. But I will always remember that Zeyana was the first one to join the fight. And that it was her wisdom that forged a new plan when the old one was shut out with the welded iron gate. It was not warmth that Zeyana shared with me. But it was strength and wisdom, and it will be sorely missed.

As we learned only recently, this wasn't the case for every member of our group. As the final placements were being made, Willa shared that she would be going south with Zeyana. The details of their relationship remained private, like so much else surrounding Zeyana, but from the subtle looks and touches between them, we can see that it is something tender. I am glad for them.

On this last night, we gather around on our pallets one last time. We cannot talk of The Traveling or impending farewell, but we can talk of our love for one another.

"When I first got here," Gemi starts, "my breasts were still full of milk. The longing for my baby pulled on my heart like an anchor, and I wanted to let it drag me down, to give into the grief and let it take me under. But Pru, you pulled me through it. You helped me wrap my breasts and gave me a poultice to stop the milk from coming. You told me that I had to be strong for my baby. You said, 'Your daughter is not an orphan, and you will not make her one. You love her too much to do that.' I can't tell you how many times I've said those words to myself these years. They've gotten me through. You all have gotten me through." She stops then to look at each of us, lingering on each face so that we understand.

Willa speaks next. "I was only sixteen when they sent me here for refusing to marry a man more than four times my age. I was so angry. Angry at my father for giving me up. Angry at Krister for not coming back for me. Angry at the whole world for being such a cruel place. If it weren't for you, Pru, I think I would have lost myself to that anger. But you took me in. You showed me kindness and reminded me that for all the cruelty in this world, there's goodness too. And each of you has shown me kindness in a different way. Gemi, your unstoppable love for your daughter. Abras, your humor and your light, even though you were born right here in this darkness. Onaris, your need to protect others, even when it cost you your own freedom. And Cala, well…" She pauses there and nods her head to me, and I nod back in understanding. "You all make me better, make the world better. I don't know who I'd be without you."

Onaris puts his arm around Willa. "Your path would have led you to goodness and light whether we were on it or not. But I'm glad we were. When I was sentenced to live out my years in the mine, I could not have imagined the beauty that I would find here. And I thank each of you for that."

"You all are a bunch of saps, going on like this," says Abras, but he's crying right along with the rest of us. "But what can you do? Family's family," he says, smiling through his tears.

I take his hand and place it in my lap. "I can't... I won't be able to say the things I want to say," I tell them. "But I will. In another life. In another world, I will tell you. For now, just know that I am grateful far more than I can say."

They all smile at me, and there's an understanding between us that doesn't take words to make clear. We are people who came together in a place that would see us fall. A place that would tell us we are nothing. But we saw each other, saw the people beyond the worn bodies. And when we forgot who we were, we reminded each other. And when our own stories became faded and distant, we told them to each other. And when a way out shone through it all, we fought like hell beside each other to get there. And now here we are, the night before the end, and the two-sided path of hope and grief is laid out before us.

"Well, we all better get some sleep," says Granna. "It would seem we are to travel tomorrow, and we shall need all of our strength," she pauses to give us one of her winks. "But before we do, I'll say one last thing. I have grown old in these mines. Some might say, I have missed out on a life. In some ways I have. But because of you, I have had love. And I have had laughter. And impossibly, I have had joy. Some might live their whole lives on the outside of these walls and never know the life I've had. So for that, I thank each of you."

We are crying again. Crying at the miracle of love and laughter and joy amidst such despair. Crying because we will part ways tomorrow. Crying because to hope is a great risk, as even greater misery might be waiting just on the other side of it.

But oh, I hope it's not. I hope that more love and laugher and joy are just on the other side of it. Because these people have endured enough. They deserve their stories. And if fortune shines down on us tomorrow, they will get them.

***

We wake to pouring rain. The mud floor of the yard oozes and squishes beneath our feet as we line up for the count. From here we can see the wagons lined up, waiting to carry us away. They are covered wagons, with a sheet of canvas pulled taught over bowed reeds. The plan is for the bulk of the guards to occupy the first two wagons, followed by two wagons of supplies, designed to be a buffer to block their view from the line of wagons behind them, which will begin to peel away from the line shortly after their departure.

The slaves will have their feet chained, and there will be one of the mine's guard's plus one Servant posing as Lord Claremont's man in each wagon as well as one driving. Once each wagon approaches its turn-off point, beginning with the last wagon and working forward, the Servant will knock out the guard, grab his keys, and then toss him out of the wagon before turning onto the designated route. At that point, the Servant will do his best to explain to the shocked travelers why he just knocked out the guard and is now unlocking their chains.

The explosions will come later. I regret not being able to see the mines destroyed, but we must wait until the wagons are safely out of the city. At nightfall, Haviel will let in a group of Servants who will sweep through the old and new mine, detonating the fire powder we have dispersed along with the ropes of tilla grass we have run throughout the mines.

As I stand in the yard, sinking into the mud, I am preoccupied with fear that they will delay the trip on account of the weather, so I fail to notice the guard approaching us through the sheets of rain.

"You two," he says, pointing to me and Onaris. "Get in that line. High profile slaves are riding up front with us. Orders from the top."

I dare not make eye contact with Granna or Abras before I turn to follow the guard. All of my concentration must be spent keeping the surging panic from registering on my face. So with eyes cast downward, I dislodge my feet from the mud and follow the guard.

***

We are settled into the wagon. It is Onaris and me and one other slave — the one who grabbed Abras's wrists that day in line. I have since learned that he goes by Chard and that he is notorious for starting fights, slave or guard, it doesn't seem to matter.

"These three are getting wrist chains and ankle chains," says one of the three guards. I realize there are no Servants in our wagon, and my heart sinks further.

I must look especially pathetic because one of the other ones chimes in, "Don't bother putting chains on that one. She isn't going to give us any trouble, are you, girl?"

I keep my shoulders slumped and my head down as I shake my head. "No." It is a gesture of false deference I learned from Teetee. They have no idea what kind of trouble is in store.

***

I can see clipped images of the city pass by through the small opening between the wagon and the cover. The rain is now a light mist. The first wagon has already turned onto its route. Our wagon, with Granna, Abras, and several other slaves, whose destinations are in the same direction, is fourth in line. Dread seizes me as I realize I won't be on it as it turns towards the western fountain, where Sentaya and Rayon are waiting.

But suddenly in a flash of brown tunic and gray hair, I see a figure rush past the wagon. Then I hear the driver exclaim, "What in all of Urendia is that?" The horses neigh as they are pulled to a sudden halt.

"It's a slave! After her!" he shouts back to the wagon as he jumps down to pursue her.

One guard stands up. "I'll go. She's an old woman. Not getting far. You two stay here with the others."

No sooner is he out of the wagon than a sudden commotion erupts around me. In one swift motion, Chard is behind one of the remaining guards and his chained arms are up over his head. With the chain around the guard's neck, Chard pulls him into a chokehold.

The other guard is up now, trying to peel Chard off the first guard, whose face has turned red in desperation. But he can't get his hands under the chains, so the three of them are locked together in a frenzy of wills.

Onaris turns to me urgently. "Go, Cala!"

"I can't leave Granna. She came for me!" I say in a rush of anguish.

"She came to give you a chance, Cala! If you stay, you'll take that from her. Go now!"

He's pushing me out as he's speaking, and soon, I am on the ground looking back up to Onaris. Onaris hears one of the guards approaching, turns around, and lunges toward him, tackling him to the ground.

I don't know what happens next because I am gone.

***

I run through the wet cobblestone streets of the city towards the western fountain. Down alleys and back roads—sticky mud from the day's rain—each step is effortful.

I know these roads because of my trips with Teetee to the market. She would take us on a different route every time we went. She could not have known what or how, but she knew a day would come when I would need to navigate the world outside my father's house. And so it has.

My lungs are burning, but I don't slow down. I picture them waiting for me: Abras, Sentaya, Rayon. I picture Granna running from the guards, buying me time. I picture Onaris wrestling the guard to the wagon floor, keeping him from me. I will not let them down.

I keep running and send a pleading thought to the wagon fleeing westward: Wait for me. I am coming.

My legs are quivering, threatening to give out. And still I run past the business district. Past the marketplace. The fountain is just over that hill. I can make it.

"You there! Stop!" A gruff voice comes from behind me.

I duck into an alley. Whoever it is, I cannot outrun them. My only hope is to lose them in the labyrinth of back alleys that Teetee has shown me. I pray that whoever now follows cannot say the same.

I am headed north now, not westward towards the fountain. When every second counts, this knowledge is almost as agonizing as my throbbing body. But I have to lose my follower; I cannot lead him to the wagon.

When I think I've lost him, I dare to pause and check for pursuing footsteps. I do not hear them. I pray that it is safe to turn back westward. The brief pause has made me even more acutely aware of the pain. My muscles and lungs plead with me to rest. But I cannot.

The last stretch is over a hill. Unbearable. To distract myself, I remember walking up this hill with Teetee. She would pretend she couldn't make it and tell me to push her up. I would make a show of getting behind her and shoving with all my might. The distraction is working. I am almost to the top.

Somehow the descent is equally painful. My shaking legs can barely keep me upright as I pitch forward and run down. I remember how Teetee and I would run down the hill together, hand in hand and I would yell, "Creesssiiiddaaa!", so that it lasted the length of the descent.

Somehow, impossibly the fountain materializes before me. I am transfixed by the miracle of it — the water trickling down three stone circles, one larger than the next, until it pools into the basin at the bottom. I have made it.

It is only once I get closer and scan the surrounding crossroads that I understand. I am too late. The wagon is gone.

***

I stumble the last steps toward the fountain and collapse at its base. Beyond the pulsing of my body is the surging realization, I have nowhere to go. I am an outcast from my home. A fugitive from the mine. And who I was supposed to become is gone, left on a westbound wagon without me.

The despair begins to take hold when I feel a hand on my shoulder. The guard pursuing me has found me. It is over.

But then. "Cala, get up."

I look up to see Abras, framed by the sunlight, smiling down at me.

"Abras," I exhale. "You came back for me."

"Of course I did."

I try to stand up but my legs give out under me. Abras helps me to stand and settles my arm around his shoulders, holding it there with one hand. He wraps his other arm around my waist and helps prop me up.

His arm around my waist sends a warm pulse through me.

"Come on. We have to go. They cannot wait for us much longer."

"Sentaya? Rayon?"

"They are waiting. We can make it if we hurry."

So, propped up by Abras, we make our way through the last stretch of alley until it deposits us onto a side street. And I can see that we made it.

The wagon is waiting, pointed westward toward the setting sun.

Chapter 8
Elina
Arcalia: Twenty-one Years Earlier

The weeks went on. I trained in the morning. I assisted Trina in the afternoons. Soon I had witnessed another kill and then another. A merchant who became too great a competition to others in Arcalia. And then a husband whose father-in-law did not like the way he treated his daughter. With each new contract, the details felt muddier and muddier.

Was this ridding the world of some cruelty? Did these men deserve to die?

But I learned to beat back the questions. The contract is the only creed. The mark is the only mission. I said these words as I trained, as I washed the dishes, as I fell asleep, as I shadowed Trina on kill after kill.

I no longer laughed with Ricard. I no longer cried to Auntie Cook. I no longer told Yera the fears within my heart.

I spent all my training hours outdoors with Yera where she taught me how to harness the predatory instincts of the dirawolf. Bare your teeth. Corner your prey. Go for the throat.

I began to earn a reputation on the sparring mat, and soon the others began to protest when they were matched against me. It was only at Smitts's unrelenting command that I had any opponents at all.

Trina began trusting me more with the planning, and I learned to collect information and construct detailed plans in a perfunctory way. Eventually, the people faded away and became merely marks. A sense of peace settled over me. Or if not peace, numbness.

I would be a dirawolf. Whether I was one or I was made into one didn't matter. It was the path I would forge for myself. And it was a path I would walk alone.

***

Months later, on a blustery autumn morning, Master Sera summoned me to her office.

"Elina, please, sit." I did. "Trina reports that you have come quite a long way."

"Thank you, Master Sera."

"I find myself curious. How did you manage to do it?"

"Manage to do what, exactly, Master Sera?"

"How did you manage to bury who you are?"

Her eyes narrowed as she searched my face, looking for a sign of doubt beneath my placid exterior. She would find none.

"I did not bury myself. I just unearthed who I was all along."

Her narrow gaze lingered a moment before her expression softened slightly.

"Well, I am glad to hear it." She paused for a beat and then went on. "As you know, you are a month away from the completion of your apprenticeship. It is time for your final test: your first contract as an assassin. As it is your first kill, you will have a full month, your remaining month as an apprentice, to prepare. Here is your contract."

She handed me a piece of parchment with a name, location and date.

"His name is Sumel Haren. He is twelve years old."

She paused again, observing. I said nothing, my eyes tracing the letters of his name.

She rose. "The contract is the only creed."

I rose in reply. "The mark is the only mission."

***

"There is no room for error, Elina. I will regain my status as senior apprentice."

"I am well aware of what's at stake, Trina," I countered.

"Go through the plan again."

I sighed. "The mark reads every evening on a bench in the southern garden of his father's estate. I will climb over the garden wall where the silberry tree grows right alongside it. Scale the branches that extend over the wall and then lower myself down on the other side with a rope. Approach the bench from behind. Slit his throat without him ever knowing I am there. Climb back up the rope and escape the same way I came."

"Right. Now let's practice your rope tying again."

***

Sumel was the first-born son of a wealthy landowner who was gravely ill. The contract came from the landowner's second wife, whose son stood next in line to inherit her dying husband's fortune.

"You are destroying who he will become," Yera reminded me as the day approached. "Young boys grow into cruel men, Elina."

But I did not need reminding any more.

***

On the night of the kill, it was custom for all of the assassins to gather to send off an apprentice to her first mark. They would continue the festivities while the apprentice was out on the job, and then she would return to a raucous celebration to honor her success.

The assassins — the same people that once shamed me as a 'worm' as Master Sera instructed — gathered in the parlor to honor me now. But my first kill wasn't about any of them, Master Sera included.

It was about becoming who I was meant to be. The kill would finalize my transformation. It would make me whole.

"Tonight, we gather to honor Elina, who leaves us an apprentice only to return an assassin."

The assassins stomped their feet twice in unison, a thunderous affirmation to Master Sera's words.

"Having proven herself worthy, she will be welcomed into our guild, and we will call her our sister."

Two more thunderous stomps.

"Go forth, Elina. Shed the fears and doubts of your past life. Embrace the certainty of the assassins' way."

Two more stomps.

"The contract is the only creed."

"The mark is the only mission," I boomed alongside the other assassins.

Now the assassins erupted into a continuous round of stomping feet, which I gathered was my send off.

***

It was several hours by horseback to reach the mark's estate. The steady rhythm of the horse's gallop became the beat as I silently chanted the words of the assassins' motto over and over until there was no beginning and no end.

We guided the horses to the woods that bordered the estate and tied them off then crept toward the silberry tree, which we had marked with white chalk for easy recognition in the fading evening light.

Trina waited at the base of the tree as I began to scale the branches. Approaching the top of the wall, I slowly pulled myself up and scanned the garden. A lantern beside the bench illuminated the silhouette of a seated figure.

This was it.

I tied the tarpin knot, securing the rope to the thickest branch that extended over the garden wall then descended silently into the garden.

I crept towards the bench, close enough that I could see the pages of his book sprawled open across his lap.

A few more silent strides and I would be within arms' reach. Suddenly, I heard steps coming from within the house. Another figure holding a lantern emerged onto the veranda.

Though I crouched behind a nearby bush, concealed by darkness, it would only take one flash of a lantern, and I'd be exposed.

"You forgot your cloak, my love. I thought you might be cold."

The figure approached the bench, and with the combined light of their lanterns, I could make them both out more clearly. Approaching the mark was a middle-aged woman, her hair pulled back to the nape of her neck. She gently placed the back of her hand against his cheek and looked down at him with an adoring smile. He lifted his head up from his book for the first time to glance up at her. Though I could only see the back of his head, I could tell that they held each other's gaze for a few moments.

"Thank you, Mother. I suppose I am a little cold."

She placed the cloak gingerly around his shoulders then rubbed them, as if bringing warmth back into him.

"What are you reading, my love?"

"A high sea adventure to discover new lands. Can you imagine it, Mother? Setting your eyes on land that no person has ever seen before? Do you suppose there's any land left like that?"

She laughed sweetly. "If there is, you'll find it." She kissed his head. "Just a bit longer, my love. Come in for bed before too long."

"I will, Mother. Just one more chapter."

"One more chapter, my love." She turned to go back inside.

Her tenderness hung in the air like a dream. And I realized it was my dream. It was the voice and the touch that I had wished my mother would use with me, the one that I felt with certainty she had used with Pru.

I imagined the tender words and touches that my mother might have offered Pru so easily as she taught her the names of plants. The way she might have laughed sweetly at Pru's innocence.

And I thought of how that tenderness had been robbed of them — for Pru, yes — but for my mother, too. How it had chilled into a hardened thing.

With one slice of my knife, I would rob the mark — this boy — and his mother of that same tenderness.

"Wait!" My voice cut into the darkness before I had even formed the thought to speak.

The mother spun around in alarm as the boy sprung to his feet and looked in the direction of my voice. Her one arm was around her son, protectively, the other thrusting the lantern toward me, its light her only defense.

"Who's there?" she demanded, the sweetness in her voice transformed into a sudden fierceness.

"Your son is in danger. I've been hired to kill him."

I could hear rustling from the silberry tree. Trina. She would not let this fail.

"What? Who…" the mother was saying.

"There isn't any time! Take your son. Get him someplace safe. Go. Now!"

They turned to run. I heard Trina land. I spun around to face her, knife drawn.

"What are you doing?" she hissed.

"I won't let you hurt him."

She lunged for me, but I expected it. I stepped to the side, and then spun around to grab her from behind.

"I'm sorry, Trina." These were my final words to her as I rendered her unconscious.

***

Returning to the Assassins' Guild, Trina draped unconscious upon her horse, I could hear the raucous celebration from within as they awaited the return of an assassin who would never come. Now, their gathering served me in a different way. It ensured that I would be able to avoid running into any of them as I planned my next move.

I guided the horses back to the stables and quickly fed and watered them. I thanked Trina wryly for helping me to perfect the tarpin knot as I used it to tie her wrists to a barn post. Then I buried her knife in a pile of hay for good measure.

As my mind raced, my feet took over, moving me steadily toward the one person who could help me.

In the kitchen, I lingered at the doorway for a moment, watching Auntie Cook bustling around the kitchen, preparing trays of food for the party.

"I didn't do it."

She spun around, one hand holding a meat tartine, the other clutching her chest.

"Elina!" She stood for a moment, drawing a few steadying breaths while she recovered from the shock. "Oh, my dear. You've saved your soul, but I fear you've put your very life in danger."

"I know. But I just couldn't do it."

She smiled at me, her warmth instantly piercing through the cold distance that I had created all these months. "No, I suppose you couldn't."

"I don't know where to go. If I go home, they will know where to find me, and I can't put my parents in danger."

Her brows furrowed as she considered my situation. Then she picked up the tray of meat tartines and strode toward the door of the kitchen.

"Stay here. Keep out of sight."

Before I could ask her any more questions, she was gone.

As I sat by the kitchen hearth, floating in the space between my unexpected choice and my uncertain future, the most surprising feeling settled over me: peace.

***

I lifted my head as I heard footsteps approaching down the hall then the swishing sound of Auntie Cook's apron. Soon she emerged in the door frame, blocking the small figure behind her.

"Looks like you are the anterlope after all."

Auntie Cook had made her way back into the kitchen, revealing Yera standing behind her, a full sack slung over each of her shoulders.

"You'd best get moving, dearies," Auntie Cook called as she busied herself with the food. "A dirawolf den is no place for an anterlope."

"Where are we going?" I asked.

"I'm taking you to my people in the Tunic Mountains," Yera said.

"But surely the assassins won't welcome you back if you help me, Yera! I can't let you do that."

"Eh, I've had about enough of this place. I can find my own way to pluck out the weeds of this world. Besides, I miss my mountain," she said decisively. "I will be sad to leave this one, though." She nodded toward Auntie Cook.

Auntie Cook called back, "Now you two don't give another thought to me." But I could hear the emotion as she choked back tears.

We strode to Auntie Cook in unison and hugged her from behind. It took both of our outstretched arms to reach all the way around her. She took each of our hands in one of hers and gave them a soft squeeze.

"Here, take some of this food." She began wrapping a tartine in a cloth. "They're too drunk to miss it. Now, go."

I took my sack from Yera and the food from Auntie Cook. We ascended the cellar steps that led to a back entrance of the manor.

The cold night air was sharp as it hit my face, and I suddenly felt that I had been holding my breath for as long as I could remember. Now, I could finally breathe.

Chapter 9
Cala
Urendia to Arcalia

The wagon from The Traveling carries us well into the night until we arrive at a small farming village on the outskirts of the city. There we meet two farmers with their carts emptied and waiting.

We climb down out of the wagon — Sentaya, Rayon, Abras and me — plus six others whose journeys will continue north-west from here to a remote village on the border between Urendia and Cantura, where a dairy farmer has offered the loft in his barn.

"I wish it were more," I say to the six. "But it is a start."

"It is everything," an older woman named Mara offers. "You have given us everything."

A few others nod. But some just stare at the ground or off into the distance. It is a lot to suddenly find your reality so substantially altered. People respond to such a thing in any number of ways.

"When some time has passed, we can help you get word to your families," Mathius, the Servant from our wagon, says to the six. "For now, you'll have a warm place to sleep and food in your bellies. Graman is a kind man."

"We best get a move on," the driver says. "Mathius, I'll go unhitch the wagon and meet you back here with the horses." And with a 'git git', he is gone.

Mathius turns to us now. "Haras, here, will get you to the border with Arcalia. From there, you'll have to find your own way." He hands us a pack. "Here's some bed rolls and a few provisions. You all better move out. No telling how much time we have before all sorts of trouble will be at our backsides."

We all mutter our words of gratitude, which can never be enough to thank someone who risked his life to save ours.

We turn to the farmer, Haras, a middle-aged man with an equal number of lines etched around his eyes from worry as creases around his mouth from smiling.

"You'll need to lay down here in the cart," he says. "I'll have to cover you with the canvas so it looks no different than taking the harvest to market. I put some straw down, but I'm afraid you're in for a bit of a stiff ride."

We put the bed rolls on top of the straw and lie down. Haras pulls the canvas up over us, blocking out the gray morning light. Soon the cart begins moving, and as the fears and worries from the overnight escape fade, we are lulled to sleep by the motion of the cart and the warmth of our tangled bodies.

We find ourselves with the open land of a foreign kingdom laid out before us and only Granna's faded recollection to help guide us to a farm where we don't know if we'll be welcome.

I should be overtaken by fear, but too many competing emotions drive it out. The thrill of the adventure before us and the start of my new story. Sheer disbelief that the plan that we worked and reworked for the better part of year actually happened. Hope that the other wagons safely reached their meet-up locations and that the people within them were now on their way to refuge. And of course, underpinning it all, grief and guilt that Granna and Onaris may not have made it out so that I could.

The others seem equally lost in their own swirling emotions when Abras pulls us all back.

"Well, shall we?"

***

The reality of our journey soon becomes clear. Haras has left us at a remote location along the border to allow for a discreet entry into Arcalia. From here, Granna told us that we would travel westward for two days through a dense forest until we arrived at a small trade road that follows the forest north-west to a trading village called Anterra. We would continue on the trade road for several more days north-westward to Galendale, the city at the heart of the kingdom. Granna's family's farm is on the outskirts of the city, another day's travel.

When Granna explained the details of the journey, pieced together from what she could remember and the rest filled in by The Servants, it sounded like a grand adventure. With Granna's knowledge of the kingdom and Onaris's experience in the world outside the mine, I imagined the four of us embarking on an exciting adventure with two very capable guides.

At first, the fresh air and freedom propel us forward with vigor. The lushness and life of the forest quenches our cracked souls after the drought of our time in the mine. But after a few hours of trekking through an overgrown forest, we have lost sight of the sun and thus our bearings. Our feet are blistered from treading over the littered forest floor and our arms are scraped from pushing past branches, with angry barbs and thorns. We drank more than the day's ration of water from our goatskin pouches. It quickly becomes apparent that while we are all survivors in our own right, none of us is particularly equipped for this journey.

All our spirits begin to dampen. All except Rayon, that is. Rayon is finally living the adventure that he daydreamed of all those years, and he is alive in a way that I've never seen him.

When one of us, overcome by weariness, begs the group to stop, Rayon — still more boy than man — declares, "In the name of the Kingdom Cressida, we must press on!" We smile and find the strength to keep going.

At several points, he climbs a tree, pulls back the top branches to reveal the sun, and redirects us slightly so we are back on our westward route. He is tireless and spirited, and I understand more fully that the weight of my father's house was shackles. And now, Rayon is casting them off and walking freely for the first time.

***

Our camp this first night is a fumbling, imprecise operation. The bed rolls we can manage. From there, we find some rope, a canvas sheet, a few flint rocks, and some dried tilla grass, whose use we know quite well. After a few failed attempts, we manage to secure the rope around three trees and drape the canvas over the top as a sort of shelter.

Next, we set about starting a fire. We learn quickly that we have to search for dry wood beneath the top layer of the forest floor, still damp from yesterday's rain, which must have swept through here as well. Could that have only been yesterday? I think back to the moment in the mine yard when the guard gestured toward the front wagon, and our plan began to come apart at the seams.

"Cala!" Sentaya chides. "Hold the rock still or I'm going to bash your hand. Then where will we be?"

I apologize and we try again to start the fire. Each spark is a tiny hope, but none ignites into anything more. By now, Rayon and Abras return, holding up their near empty water pouches to reveal that they haven't been successful in their task either.

"Pru said there'd be a river snaking along our path through this forest, but there's no sign of it," says Abras.

"We'd have pushed out a bit further, but we were afraid we might not find our way back," offers Rayon, still basking in the adventure.

"Well, we haven't had much more luck with the fire," says Sentaya. "I think the wood is just too damp. We're getting sparks, but nothing's taking."

Before the group can descend into despair, Rayon lifts us back out.

"Well, we put in half a day's journey today, so that leaves another day and half, right? If fortune shines on us tomorrow, we find the river. If she doesn't, we can stretch out the remaining water until we get to Anterra."

"What about the fire?" asks Sentaya.

"Well, we'll just have to count ourselves lucky that we are making the trek in late spring and not the height of winter," says Rayon. "We will be cold tonight, but if we huddle for warmth, we will be okay."

My face flushes at the thought of huddling for warmth with Abras. I speak up before my thoughts take me much further. "Rayon is right. We have what we need. There's enough bread and cheese left for tomorrow if we ration it out. We've certainly managed with less in the mine."

With that, Sentaya and Rayon cock their heads in twin curiosity. "What was it like in the mine?"

We settle onto our bed rolls, huddling together for warmth with our wool blankets pulled tight around us, and we do what we've done so many times before when we had nothing else. We tell our stories.

***

Abras tells them about being born in the mines and losing his mother to them. He tells how Pru, our grandmother, looked after him.

"I never told you this story, Cala, but there was this time — I must have been ten or so — when I got into a fight with this bigger kid. He called me a 'child of the mine' since I didn't really have a father, and I was born in the mine. By that point, I didn't have a mother either. It just set me off. I jumped on his back and wrapped my arms around his neck. I kind of lost it."

He pauses, transported back to the moment. We are already huddled together as closely as possible, so I lift my cheek to his in comfort. He presses his cheek back into mine.

"Well, like I said, he was much bigger, so it didn't take him much effort to fling me to the ground. Then he was down on top of me, punching me. I curled up into a ball and tried to protect my head as best I could, but he landed quite a few blows before the guards pulled him off.

"I hobbled back to our quarter, where Pru found me and patched me up, like she does."

Grief clutches at my heart as I remember Granna's capable hands, tending to my wounds after that first day in the new mine. I wish so much that she were here.

"When she was done, she lifted my chin so we were eye to eye," Abras continued. "'Abras,' she said, 'people will always find a way to lift themselves up by putting you down. That boy in the yard will see you as a child of the mine as sure as the world will see us as slaves. But you are not a child of the mine. And I am not a slave. I am Prusia Sida, and I am a healer of bodies and souls. You are Abras Cantilla, and beyond that, you are whatever you choose to be.'

"Her meaning grew as I did, and as I got older, I understood more and more what she meant. I may be forced to labor in those mines, but I could determine who I was."

"They could take your body, but they could never take your heart," I say. The gravity of Granna's own words now weigh so heavy. They had claimed her body from me. And with it our story on the farm at the base of a mountain. The tears come then, and they continue for some time, as my family holds me in warmth and in comfort.

After I'm emptied of my tears, I tell them the story of my year in the mine. That first night when I met

Granna and how much she wanted to hear about the family. The story of my father. And how The Servants and my mother and Teetee conspired against him. I tell them of the plan to take down the mine and our father. And even though I have already told them what happened in the wagon and how Granna came back for me, I tell them again, because it feels right to keep talking about her.

"What about Teetee?" Sentaya wants to know.

"Father made sure that she was sent to the farthest reaches of the kingdom to do her labor," Rayon says.

"Where?" I ask. "Do you know what direction? Do you know anything about the farmer?"

"I don't know any details." Our huddled mass sways a bit as Rayon shakes his head. "The only reason I know that much is because I heard him yell it to one of his associates from in his office."

"Growl, more like," says Sentaya.

"Was it bad? After Teetee and I left?" I ask, but I'm not sure I'm ready for the answer.

"It was like something snapped in him. He was always mean and angry, but he was controlled," Sentaya begins. And even though I can't see her face in the fireless night, I can feel the sorrow seep through her words. "After that night, after he discovered that Teetee had taught you to write under his own roof, he would just pace the house, muttering these angry rants. If anyone came too close or made too much noise, he would just unleash on them. No one was spared."

"But for us, it was even worse," Rayon says. "Somehow, he saw us as some danger, and he set out to control us even more. We were last ranked permanently. We couldn't talk to anyone, and no one could talk to us. Just seeing us would set him off, and if we didn't get out of his path quickly enough…" He trails off, sparing us the details of my father's wrath.

"I'm so sorry," I say. "This was all because of me." On top of my grief for Granna, the guilt feels unbearable.

"Cala, Father is not a good man," says Sentaya. "After hearing his full story from you tonight, maybe he never had a chance. And for that, I will always be a little sad for him."

I am taken aback by how easily she extends sympathy for a man who, only a few days ago, beat her for merely being in his presence.

"But you do not bear responsibility for his actions. You must forgive yourself, Cala."

After everything, somehow my body produces more tears.

"If your father is this unhinged," says Abras. "I worry for your remaining mothers and siblings. I think we should get word to The Servants as soon as possible that they need help."

"Yes, I think you are right," says Rayon. "But if we are going to get word to anyone, we will need to get ourselves out of this forest, which will require a long journey tomorrow. It is best that we try to rest."

We nod in agreement and lean into each other the best we can. My mind darts from Granna to Teetee to my siblings still at home. Gradually, mercifully, sleep carries me away.

***

We wake to stiff limbs and empty bellies and set about rationing the remaining food and water for the last leg of the journey before we arrive in Anterra. After devouring our small portions of bread, cheese, and dried fruit, we prepare to set out.

"According to Pru," Abras says, "our path through the forest should lead us to a small trading road, which we can take the rest of the way in. If we keep a good pace, I think we should be on the road by nightfall."

I wonder if hearing Granna's name will always produce this sharp pang of grief in my stomach. Perhaps, like the pain from the mine, it will dull but never fade.

"Well, come on then! The day beckons!" Rayon resumes his plucky disposition.

The rest of our group finishes packing up our small camp, and then we depart, Rayon at the lead. Despite the same conditions as yesterday, somehow our spirits aren't quite as heavy today. Perhaps we are emboldened by surviving the night on our own. Perhaps the weight of the stories we told, huddled together in the chilly night, lightened our souls. Perhaps seeing Rayon, head high and step light, reminds us that we are free and should not squander a single moment of it.

After some time, our bodies take over and we don't have to focus so intently on each uneven step or wayward branch. We are able to settle into conversation, which distracts us from our hunger and exhaustion. After Rayon tells us some of his adventure stories and Sentaya shares gossip from the kitchen back home, I venture into a murkier topic.

"Sentaya," I start. "How can you feel anything but anger for Father?"

"What do you mean?" she asks. "I feel anger for him."

"I know, but last night, you said you felt sadness for him too. Why does he deserve your sadness?"

She ponders that for a few moments. "Do you remember those feral cats that would roam the alley behind our house?"

"Yes. One time Rayon got that big scratch on his cheek when he tried to pick one up."

"Yeah, and my two older sisters laughed all the way back to the house," Rayon adds playfully. We all laugh at the memory, and Abras joins too, no doubt imagining our trio running in the alley from feral cats.

"Well," Sentaya goes on. "Did you hate those feral cats for hissing and scratching?"

"No, I felt sorry for them. Remember we would give them names and pretend they were our pets?"

"I remember there was a striped one I named Tiger," says Rayon.

"And even though they bit and scratched, we took pity on them because we knew they didn't have homes or families."

"So that is how you see Father?" I ask.

"Kind of. I still have a lot of anger, but in some ways, I think his whole life probably made him the way he is, and I think that's sad."

"But what about Abras?" I press. "He was born in the mine just like Father, and he even lost his mother, and he's not a feral cat."

"My! Such flattery, Cala!" Abras jokes.

"You know what I mean. You had it just as hard as my father, maybe harder."

"I had Pru," says Abras.

"So did my father!" I reply.

The strange parallel between Abras and my father sinks in for a minute. How could such similar starts in life yield such different outcomes?

"Cala, do you remember when we were really little, and we found that gray cat?" Sentaya asks.

"No," I say.

"We were very small. And the cat didn't hiss or scratch. It let us come near. And though it was a little afraid, eventually I was able to pet it. I wanted to bring it home, but the mothers said no."

"I have a fuzzy memory of you wailing in the garden about a mouse," I offer.

189

"Mouse! Yes, that's what I named it because it was gray. It was so sweet and gentle, even though it had no home or family."

"Why?" It's Abras who wants to know this time.

"I don't entirely know," Sentaya says. "But what the cat, Mouse, shows is that, it's not just about what you face in life; it's also about what you had inside you to begin with. Mouse had a gentleness about him that couldn't be broken by living on the street."

"And you have a kindness that couldn't be broken by the mine, Abras," I say as I reach for his hand and squeeze it.

"And Father?" Rayon wonders.

"Father had a weakness that was only made worse by the mine. Maybe he would have been different if he had had a different start. We will never know. And I am angry, Cala. I am angry that he made us all quiver with fear in our own house. That he ranked his own children then cut us off from our family. That he turned in his own wife and daughter and condemned them to years of suffering." She pauses for a moment, takes a small breath, and then resumes more softly. "But I'm sad for him too. How awful it must be to be a monster."

Sentaya finishes, and the wisdom of her words pushes up against the anger in my heart.

"I can't let go of the anger," I say quietly.

It is Abras now who shares his wisdom. "You may yet, Cala. You may yet."

"And besides," Sentaya continues. "I take some satisfaction in knowing that I got a little revenge."

We all stop and turn to face Sentaya at the back of the line. She reaches into the satchel at her side and produces a leather pouch. She gives it a little shake so that we can hear the chink chink of the coins within. And just when I was beginning to think that Sentaya had completely transformed into a wise and pious woman, I see her lips curl into her mischievous grin.

"Pity or not, I think it was the very least Father could do for us, don't you?"

"Surely, he wouldn't want his own children to starve," I add wryly.

She puts the pouch back into the satchel, and we resume our trek.

Just before dusk, the dense forest suddenly starts to open then empties us onto a cart-trodden dirt road.

"The trading road!" Rayon shouts and jumps into the air, arm raised, expelling a little, "Whoop! Whoop!"

Despite ourselves, we join him, whooping. And then we hug and jump together in a little circle. Joy and relief sweep through me, a welcome change from the other emotions that have been swirling these past days.

We decide to trek back into the forest to set up camp, allowing the thick trees to offer some cover. Luckily, our wood has dried enough to start a fire. We sit around it, entertaining Abras with stories of our childhood antics. We laugh until we hold our sides then settle onto our bed rolls to sleep, the warmth of the waning fire at our backs.

One by one, the breathing of the others begins to slow and settle into soft snores, but my mind wards off sleep. I wonder what they've done with Granna. Is she back in the mine? Is she in the stockades? Is she cold or hurt or hungry? I send her a loving thought and hope it reaches her heart.

I'm pulled from my thoughts by the sound of a nearby branch breaking, and I instantly imagine the silhouettes of kings' guards closing in on us. I stiffen and panic begins to take hold when I hear Abras whisper, "Cala, are you awake?"

"Yes, but you scared me out of my wits!"

"I'm sorry," he says, sounding as though he is smiling.

"I'll bet." I smile back.

"May I lie here?" he asks.

I scoot over on my bed roll.

He lies down next to me, and the pull toward each other is a force beyond our control. Our lips touch, soft at first then hungry. For the first time, we are free to do as we please without risk of discovery. Abras and I had become expert at finding stolen moments these past few months. But now, the whole night stretches before us; our whole lives stretch before us. And the freedom is intoxicating. Our bodies are our own, and they are each other's.

Chapter 10
Elina
Arcalia: Twenty-one Years Earlier

After the first night amongst the Tunic people, when Yera and I collapsed into a tent with exhaustion, it was a tribal decision as to whether I would be allowed to stay any longer. That second night, the elder council convened, and the whole tribe gathered around to listen. The elders asked me question after question until my story was laid bare in front of the entire tribe. It was difficult to tell it, but once the words were freed into the night, I felt light with relief.

After listening to my story and discussing the situation well into the night, the elders made a proposal. I would be welcomed into the tribe as a child because my childhood had been stolen from me. Along with the children of the tribe, I would learn tanouli and discover my kimbasa. I would be reborn.

As was custom with major decisions, the elder council made their proposal and then every member of the tribe, many hundreds of people, including the children, got to cast their vote. I watched as each person walked up to the elder counsel table to place a pebble in one of two bowls. It was an extraordinary thing to witness, seeing every single person be counted. It was something that I had never seen before, not at The Assassins' Guild, not in Arcalia, and certainly, not in my own family.

I watched in awe and some trepidation, knowing that my fate would be determined by the will of a people whom I had never met, who owed me nothing. But person by person, pebble by pebble, they voted to welcome me in, to begin my childhood anew.

When it was over, the elders officially welcomed me into their tribe by giving me my own pebble and a new name, Havita, which means child of peace.

***

As a child of the tribe, I would learn right alongside the rest of the children. Akita was my teria, my guide, but he was not my teacher. The only true teacher in the ways of tanouli is nature herself. But a guide can show you the way, help you to see what your eyes may have otherwise been closed to.

Growing up nestled at the base of a mountain, I was no stranger to nature. I had found respite in our meadow and up the mountain and welcomed the space to move and think freely.

But tanouli is not simply an appreciation or even love of nature. It is a connection with nature deep within your soul, as Yera had first explained it to me in the garden at The Assassins' Guild so many months ago.

What I came to understand in my short time on the mountain is that tanouli is as much about discovering yourself as it is about discovering nature. You have to look inward to discover your place in nature. Not all people connect with nature in the same way. And so, you must understand who you are first. Then you can discover your kimbasa, your kindred animal, and from there your place in nature.

And so, some months later, it was on this inward journey that I found myself with Akita, and a herd anterlope.

"There." Akita pointed across the tall grasses of the meadow to a large brown and black anterlope standing prominently away from the herd. "That's the leader. You can tell from the size of the horns."

Two perfect spirals ascended toward the sky.

"Why is he standing away from the herd like that?" I ask.

"She."

"It's a female?"

"Anterlope are one of the few animals where females can grow horns," Akita explained. "She is protecting the herd. See how they are grazing with their heads down and their tails swishing? They are not on high alert. She is."

"She is their protector."

"If the herd is in danger, she will alert them, and then they will take a defensive formation."

"I didn't know that females could be herd leaders."

"It is not common, but I believe that they make better leaders. They are mothers. They protect with a mother's heart."

"Not all mothers have a protective heart," I said, more to myself than Akita. But Akita knew my story, so he took in my words with deep consideration.

"You don't believe your mother had a protective heart?" Akita probed in his gentle way.

"I didn't feel protected. I felt abandoned."

"That is your truth." He paused, letting his validation settle for a few moments. "But what was your mother's, I wonder."

"I know what you're getting at. She did what she did to protect me. But why defend her? You all agreed: she stole my childhood!"

My voice rose in anger, and the herd of anterlope dashed off in an instant.

Akita pressed on unfazed. "I do not defend her. Your mother was wrong to do what she did. But the question is, did she do it with a protective heart?"

"What difference does it make?"

"The difference between you holding onto your anger or letting it go."

I looked away, anger giving way to sorrow. Tears began to form.

"I don't want to hold onto it, but I cannot let it go."

"It will not be easy, but you can, Havita. You will have to learn how. Achieving tanouli is impossible when anger courses through you. Only a heart at peace can connect with its kambasa." He put his hand on my shoulder kindly.

By then, I was crying in earnest, and I turned back toward the village, away from Akita and the empty clearing, where the anterlope had grazed only moments earlier. My past had dug its thorns into me, and I could not see a way forward.

**

"How did it go today?" Yera asked from her side of the tent we shared.

"Ugh," I groaned.

"It isn't meant to be easy, Elin... Havita."

"I don't expect it to be easy. But this is impossible."

"Why?"

"Because I can't let go of my anger, and according to Akita, tanouli will be impossible to achieve if I can't."

"He's right."

"How did you manage to do it?" I asked.

"Do what?"

"How did you manage to achieve tanouli while holding onto your anger toward the Arcalians?"

"I didn't."

"What do you mean?"

"I no longer have tanouli. I chose anger."

"What are you talking about? Your kimbasa is the neru. I've seen you move."

"She was my kimbasa. But when anger overtook me, I lost my connection with her. My body still remembers to move the ways she taught me, but my soul is no longer connected to hers. Once anger was my only companion, I left and joined the assassins."

"Yera, I… I don't know what to say."

"You don't have to say anything. It is not for you to understand my path. Only your own."

"Well, I don't even understand that."

"I know your path is dark, Havita. Mine has seen its share of darkness, so I do not speak to you from a place of enlightenment. But I will tell you this. I knew the peace of tanouli. Anger may be my only companion now, but it does not warm my soul the way that my kimbasa did. Consider your path carefully."

The next morning, Yera was gone before the sun was up, her pack and her anger gone with her.

***

The next morning, I silently cursed Yera as I made my way to her mother's meal tent alone.

"She's gone?" Haryana asked, searching behind me for her daughter, Yera, and then up at me for confirmation.

"Yes," I said, unable to meet her gaze.

"I'm surprised she stayed as long as she did."

"She has a lot she is still battling — inside I mean."

Haryana nodded.

"Is it all right that I still sit here?" I asked, nodding down to one of the two empty mats on the floor of her meal tent.

"What, because Yera left? Yes, I hope you will. I'm happy to have somebody to feed."

"Thank you," I said, smiling.

She offered me some of her dried meat and wild berries, which I gratefully devoured.

"I gather you're having a bit of trouble," she said, lovingly cutting to the point as only a mother could.

"You could say that."

"It's a hard thing, learning tanouli at your age. For children, it is easier. Their hearts are not weighed down by pain. There is less to get in the way of the connection."

She looked into my eyes for a few moments, as if seeing something there. I looked away, self-consciously. What did she see?

"Havita, there is someone I think you should know." She stood up and began clearing the food.

"But I must get to the meadow, or I will miss the lesson."

"Perda will offer you lesson enough."

The abrupt change of plan left me unsettled, but I did not feel that I was in a position to protest the person who fed me, especially not on the same morning her daughter had left without so much as a goodbye. So I helped Haryana clean up then followed her to meet Perda. As we walked the path away from the village, I was surprised to feel a little flicker inside my chest: hope.

***

Most of the village sprawled across a clearing at the mouth of the great pine forest. But some dwellings stretched into the forest, popping up at random amidst the towering trees.

It was here that we found Perda, whom I recognized as one of the elders from the council, hunched over a pack. She rose in greeting, and I took in her shriveled copper skin and silver hair, pulled back into a coarse braid down her back. She must have been at least seventy, but her eyes danced with youth and vigor.

"Ah, Havita," she said, eying me with the same intensity that Haryana had earlier.

"Perda," Haryana began. "I believe Havita would do well from spending some time with you."

"I can see that," Perda said in reply. I wasn't sure how to take that. "She can come along. I'm trekking to the peak."

"A good morning for it."

"How long does it take to trek to the peak?" I asked, glancing toward the mountain top, even though it was obscured by the pines from here.

"A day on my own. With you two."

I laughed at the thought that I'd slow down this old woman, but a stern glance from both transformed my laughter which trailed into an awkward throat clearing.

"Oh, well, I haven't prepared for a trek, and I really shouldn't miss the lessons."

"I've got another pack inside my tent. You have what you need. We will leave shortly."

***

We began our ascent up the zigzagging trail, largely overgrown. Every step required careful attention so as not to lose my footing. To my left, I could reach out to the branches that jutted out from the side of the mountain for support when I needed it. To my right, there was a cliff, over the edge of which I kicked sticks and pebbles and dirt as I fumbled — taking no comfort in the fact that I could not hear them hit the bottom.

Meanwhile, Perda seemed to know every step of this mountainside by heart. She stepped blindly and easily over each divot or root, which left her eyes free to scan our surroundings. She would occasionally point to a wilderbeast grazing along the mountainside or a brush hawk circling above us. I found her graceful movements and cheerful disposition utterly irritating as I tried not to trail too far behind.

By mid-morning, my feet were throbbing, and I was desperate to sit down.

"Looks like you could use a rest," she said.

Perda led me to a trickling stream, where I sat to unlace my boots, well-worn from my days on the farm.

"Those heavy boots are weighing you down," she said as a statement of fact.

"I suppose so. They're the only shoes I own."

I put my aching feet in the cool stream and groaned audibly.

"You need to move more lightly."

I glanced at her shoes, soft leather stitched together to fit the shape of her feet.

"Well, what do you propose, we trade shoes?" I asked irritably.

She laughed, apparently finding my ill-temper amusing.

"You can tie yours together and carry them over your shoulder. I'll give you mine to wear, and I will walk barefoot."

"You're going to walk barefoot up a mountain?" I eyed her incredulously. "What if you step on something?"

"This mountain would do me no harm. No more harm than those boots are doing to you anyway." She laughed again.

I did not.

She tossed me a pouch with pumpkin seeds. "Eat some of those and let the water soothe your feet for a stretch. Then we will continue on."

Apparently, her idea of a stretch was different from mine. In what felt like mere moments, she sprung to her feet with impossible energy for a seventy year old. I slowly eased her shoes onto my aching feet and stood up, hissing in pain as they bore my weight again.

Perda laughed again. "Come on then. The peak awaits." And with that, she ducked through the brush back toward the mountain trail.

"The mountain thanks you for not crushing it with the weight of your boots any longer!" she called back from the thick of the brush.

"Well, you can tell the mountain you're welcome." Except then a branch whipped me across the face. "Oh, never mind!"

***

Perda's shoes were an improvement. The thin leather souls were light on my feet, but there was something more. Now, I could feel the trail beneath me, so my feet registered the divots and roots that had sent me stumbling earlier that morning.

"Better?" Perda called.

"Yes, actually."

"I was talking to the mountain."

"Oh."

"You two seem to be in agreement."

"Glad to hear it."

The day wore on, and my body and mind fell into rhythm navigating the mountain trail. The stepping, dodging, grabbing became a sort of dance that felt less and less fumbling and more and more graceful. It still required all of my focus to ascend the mountainside without stumbling, but there was a lightness to it now.

I was surprised when I looked up at one point to see the sun descending into the horizon and the light taking on a new shadowy quality.

"We will stop ahead."

I had learned by then not to respond as Perda spoke to the mountain more than me.

"Havita?"

"Oh, yes, fine."

Perda led us away from the mountain-edge trail, to a large clearing with a firepit in the middle.

"My people come here for the moon bath celebration."

"Moon bath celebration?"

"When the moon is at her roundest and brightest, we come here to bathe in her light."

I glanced up at the cloudy night sky, trying to imagine what the clearing would look like bathed by the moon.

"We believe that moonlight can awaken what lies dormant within. So we come here when the moon is so bright it might be daytime, and we bathe in her light to awaken us."

"What did it awaken for you?" I wondered.

"Oh, many things over the years. Most recently, it reawakened a curiosity that I had not felt since I was a child. I was suddenly curious to know a great many things, and so I began to ask. 'Why can we not sing to each other the way birds do?' 'Why must we wait until the end of the meal to eat our frita cakes when they are the most delicious part?' 'Why do we sleep when the stars shimmer across the sky so beautifully?'"

"And did you get your answers?"

"No! And so I began to sing to the others and eat my frita cake first and sit up gazing at the shimmering stars."

I was glad the darkness concealed my lips as they curled into a smile at the thought of Perda behaving like a child in her old age.

"And you think that all was awakened by the moonlight?"

"What else?" she asked, as if it was the most obvious explanation.

"I don't know," I answered truthfully.

"All right!" she exclaimed, clapping her hands. "Let's start a fire so we can cook these fish I caught while you were lazing about by the stream."

"I wasn't lazing! My feet were in pain."

"Maybe you could use those feet to gather some dry firewood?" she asked cheerfully.

Before long, Perda had gutted the fish and tended to a growing fire. Once the fish were cooked and cooling, Perda stood and held her hands, palm-up, toward the sky.

"Great mother, we have taken the fish from your stream, the wood from your forest, and the water from your sky. You nourish us with your very self, and we thank you." She held her hands up a moment longer and then glanced over to me expectantly.

I stood up, and with the same gesture, added, "We thank you." I began to sit back down, but she glanced over at me again, eyes narrowed, so I added, "And uh, sorry for walking on you with my boots."

Satisfied, Perda laughed as she sat down and handed me my plate. I was about to take a bite of the fish, when I noticed her holding a bit of frita cake and chewing with her eyes closed, a wide smile on her face. So, I picked up the piece of frita cake from my plate and took a bite, closing my eyes and smiling, too.

***

After the meal, we went about setting up our bed rolls. I curled up on mine and stared, mesmerized by the dancing flames of the fire. I began to feel myself taken by the heaviness of sleep, when Perda's voice suddenly pulled me back.

"I must have been about your age when it happened." She paused for a moment and then went on.

"My mother was gathering creya shrooms at the edge of the village when we heard her scream. My father and I dropped the hide we were stretching out and went running.

"We found her beneath a man trying to force himself onto her, pinning her against a tree. It was the first time I had ever seen someone from outside our village. His pale skin and yellow hair were almost as shocking as what he was doing to my mother.

"My father leapt on the man with a fierceness I had never seen from him. His kimbasa was a staya, a tiny songbird, and all I had known from him until that moment was gentleness. He ripped the man from my mother and threw him to the ground. But then the man pulled something from his belt, something not from our world. Soon, there was a horrifying crack, like wood splitting or thunder booming, but much greater. I did not understand what I had heard, but then I saw my father clutch his chest and fall to his knees.

"Soon others from the village arrived, and the man took off running into the woods. My father was lying on the ground now, staring with empty eyes toward the sky, as my mother sprawled over him wailing."

She paused. By then, I was sitting up and watching her as she stared at the fire, saying these words almost flatly.

"The anger that settled into me was poison. It swept through me each day and followed me into my dreams at night. I could feel nothing else. I screamed and fought and wouldn't let anyone near me. It was like that for some time."

"What did you do?" I asked, overcome with a sudden urgency to know.

"I will show you tomorrow." And then, as abruptly as she had begun, she stopped speaking, saying nothing more that night.

**

When Perda shook me awake in the early hours of the morning, my body protested fiercely. The sheer amount of effort it took to open my eyes, let alone roll out from under the blanket, was enormous. Somehow, I managed and found myself wading through the fog that blanketed the clearing. Exhaustion hung heavy as we found our way to the trail and set out on the final stretch of the mountain.

Perda bounded ahead in good spirits and prattled away to her mountain. Scrambling along behind her, I felt like a forgotten third member of the excursion.

As the fog cleared and the exertion began to wake me up, I was able to navigate the trail with less and less concentration, which left my mind free to wander. It quickly found its way back to Perda's story from last night. It was so different from the chipper old woman ahead of me — like this other thing that lived inside her.

And then, there was the promise to tell me how she moved past the anger. What would she show me today?

How was it even possible to let go of anger toward a stranger who tried to rape your mother and then murdered your father? How does such an anger not grip you until your very dying breath?

I thought then of my mother, who helplessly watched strangers carry off her daughter. A mother who turned her helplessness onto her next daughter, twisting it, forging it into something damnable. Forging me into something damnable.

She was far from the villain in Perda's story. And yet, Perda could let go of her hatred toward that villain. It was unfathomable.

Before long, the ascent required my full attention again, and my thoughts receded, unresolved. The trail grew steeper, and I had to pitch forward to keep my balance. My breath became labored, and my legs burned from the intensity of the climb. The physical excursion was a welcome relief from my swirling thoughts.

"Just about there, Havita!" Perda called back, not out of breath in the least.

The pines began to thin and soon the flat top of the mountain, covered in vibrant green craw brush, stretched out before me.

"Hello, old friend," Perda said, tossing her pack and lying down amongst the craw brush as if she was collapsing into bed after a long time away from home. It felt intimate almost, so I decided to leave her alone.

But I couldn't wander too far, just a carved out space where I could sit and take in the view.

The green rolling peaks stretched out in front of me, giving way to pine forests, and then beyond that, the entire world seemed to go on forever. I could see land that would take days to walk to, rivers carving their way through it, and even villages popping up way off in the distance. The world took on a muted tone, as if a hazy backdrop to my own story. A surge of self-importance swept over me, but somehow, simultaneously I was struck by my insignificance.

What was my story amidst the countless others that were, at that very moment, consuming the minds and hearts of the people who scurried below me? To each of us, our story is everything. A precious thing to be held lovingly in our hands, protected and cherished and misunderstood and then, maybe, understood a little more. And then inevitably, all too soon, extinguished.

But what was I doing with my story? Was I holding it lovingly in my hands? Or was I shaking it violently, raging against its memory so that its very image became blurred?

"Havita?" The voice startled me.

"Huh!" I gasped. "Surely you know it is unwise to startle someone sitting upon a mountain's edge?"

"She held you in her grip. You would not fall." She paused, making her way down to my nook. "May I join you? I would like to finish my story."

"Yes," I said, although she had already taken the seat beside me.

She gazed out at the horizon, much the same way she did at the fire the night before. Then, she continued.

"The anger was a poison, and I was sure that it was a part of me. After some time, my mother took me up the mountain. She took me here, to this peak, where there was a wild storm, wind blowing rain sideways. She told me to give my anger to the wind, that it would carry it away from me. I laughed at her. How foolish she was. This anger was in my blood. The wind could do no such thing."

"What did she do?" I asked.

"She shook me until I was no longer laughing. I was screaming. I screamed at her for venturing out alone to collect creya shrooms. I screamed at my father for believing that he could take down a stranger with a strange weapon. But mostly, I screamed at that man. For taking everything from me. For destroying my father, the beautiful songbird, who was delicate and kind, and for poisoning me with anger. I screamed and screamed, and the wind carried it all away. And then I cried and cried. And my mother held me and cried too."

"And that was it? Your anger was gone?"

"For a time. But it came back. When a man laid an unwelcome hand on me, it came back. When my first child was born, and my father wasn't there to see him, it came back. When my mother died, and I had to say goodbye again, it came back."

"So you *were* poisoned. I knew it."

"I chose not to be. Each time I came up here, I screamed until it was all out. I gave my anger to the wind, and it carried it away. It will never be gone, Havita. But you will learn to find a way to get it out. And once you do, you will find peace."

"How?" I said, beginning to feel the familiar choking in my throat as tears forced their way out.

"You will discover your own ways, but today, I will show you mine. When Haryana brought you to me yesterday, I was coming up here to give my anger away, once again."

"Why?"

"My husband is sick. He does not have much longer. I am so angry that the world will take away another man that I love."

"I am so sorry, Perda."

"As am I. I need to grieve, but my anger is standing in the way. So here I am to let it out."

With that, she turned toward the expanse of world before us and screamed a deep and guttural scream, one filled with a lifetime of anguish. When all of the air was used up, she drew in breath and began again and again and again until her voice was hoarse, and she could scream no longer. Then, she bent forward and sobbed. It was difficult to watch, but it also felt like a privilege to bear witness to this woman, expelling such profound emotion on that mountainside.

After some time, she stood up. "Now you."

"I can't."

"Havita, you can. You are choosing to hold onto it."

"Why would I choose to hold onto this?"

"Because it is all you have of your mother, this anger; it is the only connection you feel to her, and you are afraid to let it go."

Her words pierced me with such clarity that I stumbled back into the face of the rock.

"Scream out your anger, Havita. Say what you are feeling. The wind will take it from you."

I started to mutter a bit about my mother and my childhood with little conviction then suddenly Perda was shaking me, as her mother had done to her.

"What did you feel?" she yelled.

"I felt alone!" I yelled with more vigor.

"Why?" she said, still shaking me.

"Because she left me!" I screamed more intensely.

"Why did she leave you? You were just a child!" she yelled into my face as she shook me by the shoulders.

"She left me! She left me because I was not Pru." I was hysterical now, but I didn't care. "I could not be Pru, so she destroyed who I was and turned me into something she couldn't lose. But she lost me anyway! She couldn't see past her fear. She wasn't strong enough. I needed her to be stronger! Why wasn't she stronger? Why didn't she save me?" I ran out of words, so then I was just screaming, deep and guttural as Perda had done.

Afterwards I collapsed, feeling emptied, and cried as Perda held me, as her mother did her.

"The wind will take it from us," she said finally.

Soon the craw brush shushed us gently as a wind swept through the mountain and took our anger far away.

Chapter 11
Cala
Arcalia

Traveling along the open, dusty road feels practically like floating after the day and a half laboring through the dense forest. The plan is to walk the remaining stretch along the trade road but to take cover in the forest if we hear anyone approaching. We are a few hours into the trek, and so far we have taken cover several times. Once for a farmer hauling a cart of hay bales and once for a family shepherding a flock of sheep.

Abras holds my hand as we walk, and my mind replays moments from the night before. Our lips. Our hands. Our bodies. I glance over at him, and he is looking at me. He doesn't look away. Nightfall cannot come soon enough.

Soon, we see a signpost that says 'Anterra'. By now we have used the last of our rations, so the sign announcing the outer limits of the trading town is a welcome sight. As we get closer, we see a small poster nailed to the sign.

"What does it say?" Abras asks.

We all look to Rayon. Teetee had begun teaching me my letters, but I had not yet moved past simple words.

Rayon clears his throat. *"Wanted: runaway slaves. All citizens will report suspicious figures or face imprisonment."*

Before the meaning takes full form in our mind, we hear a wagon approaching and we all dive into the woods.

Soon we erupt in a whispered argument about what to do.

"Let's just skip Anterra and keep going to Galendale," says Rayon.

"We are out of food and water, Rayon," Sentaya says in an admonishing older sister way I've heard many times before. Despite the urgency of the situation, I can't help smiling at the familiar squabbling of my siblings.

"I know that, Sentaya. But you said it's just several more days to Galendale. We can find the river for water and forage for food. Surely, there are berries and other edible things in the forest. We could even get fish from the river."

"Rayon," I say gently, hoping not to crush his spirit of adventure. "These are all things that we can learn in time, and we will! We will explore the wild fields and mountains near Granna's farm." I pause as the familiar stabbing pain seizes me. "But for now, we don't know enough to survive in the wild — which berries are safe to eat, what we can use to catch fish. We have to go into Anterra to get what we need. This was part of the plan."

"And it would seem that fortune is on our side," Sentaya added. "Given the carts and livestock we've seen coming into town, it seems that we have happened upon a market day."

"But the four of us will draw too much attention," Abras says. "As the oldest, I think I should go."

"I think a woman doing her market shopping would draw less suspicion," I say. "Not to mention, you've never been to a market, Abras. It will be harder for you to blend in."

"Fair point. So what do you propose?"

"I'll go," I say. "I'll slip in, buy a few provisions, and meet you back here by nightfall."

"I'm going with you," says Sentaya. "Two sisters at the market won't attract too much attention."

"I don't like it," says Abras. "But I think you're right. It's the best plan." He forces a smile.

Sentaya and I ready ourselves, uncrumpling the traveling clothes that we have now been wearing for almost two days. We use the last bit of water from the pouches to scrub the grime off our hands and faces and necks. As much as it pains us, we each tear a thin strip from the edge of our blankets to serve as a headscarf. It will provide a bit more anonymity, and it's customary for young women to cover their hair in public.

"Well, how do we look?" I ask.

"Like the two fairest maidens in all of Arcalia!" declares Abras.

As Sentaya empties her satchel to make room for the marketplace provisions, Abras pulls me to the side.

"Be quick and careful," he says.

"Quick and careful," I promise. "Look after Rayon. Don't let him eat any berries." We laugh softly.

"If you're not back by sundown, I'm coming after you."

Then he pulls me in and kisses me. It isn't until we pull apart again that I notice Sentaya and Rayon blushing and looking off into the woods, and it occurs to me that it's the first time we've kissed in front of them.

***

A short way down the road, Sentaya turns toward me as we walk.

"So you and Abras," she says. "When… how… did that start?"

"It's hard to say exactly. I think there was something between us from the beginning, but I didn't understand it for what it was at first. He was just so kind and made me smile. Then it just kind of slowly became more."

"I can tell he truly cares for you. That day in the wagon, I don't think we would have been able to get them to wait for you if it weren't for Abras. The driver said there just wasn't time, but Abras held him by the collar and said with such fierceness that if it weren't for you, none of this would have even happened. That we owed you everything, at the very least a couple of hours. The driver hesitated, but he listened. I'm not sure Abras would have given him a choice."

"Wow," I say, imagining Abras holding someone by the collar for me.

"Yeah. Wow." She pauses as the depth of Abras's love for me sinks in for us both then continues. "You know, I never dreamed of love. It never occurred to me to. A man just meant control and anger and hurt. I figured father would marry me off at some point, but I never imagined kindness or tenderness or devotion. You and Abras have shown me a different way."

"I wish you could have met Onaris and seen the special connection between him and Granna, the way that he considered my ideas when I spoke, and how he tipped his head in greeting to show his respect. He devoted his whole life to protecting people, Sentaya, and in the end, he protected me so I could get away."

"He sounds extraordinary," she says.

"He was… is," I say, praying that it's still true, that it's not too late for Onaris.

The foot and cart traffic begin to pick up a bit as we approach the town center.

"All right, time to get our story set," Sentaya says.

This was an art we had perfected over the years, inventing and then memorizing the details of our stories to avoid punishment after we had disobeyed the mothers. We learned to use specific details and project confidence with our delivery, and more often than not, we pulled it off. And so, like we had done so many times before, we begin to spin our story.

***

By the time we reach the town's center, it is afternoon, and many of the carts have already packed up and gone home. We make our way through the remaining goods.

Despite our surging fear, we force our bodies to move slowly, hoping to give off a leisurely feel so as not to attract attention. At three stalls, we receive no more than a nod or a brief glance as we load up on apples, bread and dried meat. We then make our way through the remaining carts, adding bundles of kindling and a bottle of goat's milk that we rest on the top of Sentaya's bursting satchel.

As we prepare to leave the marketplace — ready to return to Abras and Rayon — a hand grips my arm and spins me around.

"Haven't seen you two around here before." A gruff uniformed man peers down at our faces, still gripping my arm.

"Hello, good sir," Sentaya begins. "We are new to the area."

"New to the area, eh? We are on the lookout for some escaped slaves. You wouldn't know anything about that." He expels a thick wad of black spit, which nearly lands on my foot.

"Goodness, no!" I say, widening my eyes in mock alarm. "How dreadful."

"Indeed. And where did you say you were from then?"

"Oh, we didn't," I go on. "Our father's brother owns a dairy farm aways out, and we have come to help for the summer."

"The Breyer place?" he asks.

"Mhmm, that's the one," Sentaya chimes in casually.

"What do they need help for? They must have eight kids! Seems like enough help for one farm."

"Yes, that's just it," Sentaya goes on. "Our aunt, poor thing, has been most poorly since the last baby came along, and she just can't manage with all those children running about."

"Seemed fine the last time they came into town," the man retorts.

"Oh yes," I say. "She puts on a brave front, doesn't she? Poor thing barely wanted to admit to us that she needed help. But she's just so run down. Thank goodness we're here."

We both smile sweetly.

He nods towards our satchel. "What do you need with a bottle of goat's milk on a dairy farm?"

"Wouldn't you know, one of the children can't stomach cow's milk!" I say, pretending to be taken by the surprise of it.

"On a dairy farm, no less!" Sentaya adds in case he missed the irony of it.

"Hmmph," he snorts. "Well, you'd better get back to it."

"Especially with those dangerous runaways lurking about," Sentaya adds with concern. "Wouldn't want to get caught out after dark."

We turn to continue on our way when he speaks again.

"Aren't you two headed the wrong way? Breyer Farm is up that way," he says pointing the other direction up the main road.

"Still getting our bearings, I suppose," Sentaya says with an embarrassed laugh.

"Suppose so," he says. And then mercifully turns to continue his rounds.

We scurry up the main trade route in the wrong direction. It's a busy time of day, with people coming and going from the marketplace, and we don't dare duck into the woods lest we arouse any suspicion from those passing by. As we continue along, I eye the sun, dipping toward the horizon as late afternoon turns to early evening. The knowledge that Abras will come looking for as at sundown pulses in my mind and makes it difficult to focus. Sentaya takes my arm and guides me along.

After some time, the crowd begins to thin, and there are larger and larger gaps between travelers. As soon as we see that no one is approaching, we glance back to see the way behind us is empty as well. Without hesitation, we dive into the forest and circle back in the other direction.

The sun is low in the sky now, as we make our way through the dark forest, and we have to go more by feel than sight. We run, barely watching our step or clearing branches from our way as we race the setting sun. I hear a crashing sound behind me.

"The goat milk!" Sentaya says.

"Leave it! There's no time!"

The dark cover of the forest masks the true hour, and it's impossible to know if we are already too late. We can't do anything but press on and pray.

It takes me a moment to realize that we have passed this way before. It is Sentaya who notices. "Cala! The embers!"

She points to the fire, now barely lighting the darkness. We see our packs resting up against the trees. It is our camp. But Abras and Rayon are nowhere to be seen.

We bend over, hands on knees, catching our breath for a few moments before we can talk.

"We are too late. They must have already gone looking for us. We need to try to stop them before they get to the town."

So we circle around for the third time today, rushing back the way we came to see if we can intercept Rayon and Abras before they get to the town. Despite the danger, we run along the side of the road — the only way we can hope to catch up to them. Our legs and lungs burn, but we press on. Impossibly, it was only a few days ago that I ran toward all three of them with the same painful urgency.

By now, the moon shines down through a clear sky, illuminating the path just enough for us to see a little way ahead of us. Before long, we see two figures in the distance.

"Cala, there!" Sentaya says.

"I see, too!" I say.

We slow to a quiet stride, trying not to announce ourselves in case it is not Abras and Rayon. As we get closer, we can make out their familiar features.

"Abras! Rayon!" we call.

They turn around, their alarm dissolving quickly into relief. Our arms are around one another, and we are a mess of limbs and whispered words.

Still holding each other, we move into the safe cover of the forest before looping back, for the last time today. On the journey back, we fill them in on the run-in with the officer and how we had to trek in the wrong direction for some time.

Back at our camp, we rebuild the fire and unpack the market food. I am not sure I have ever enjoyed a meal more than that apple, bread and dried meat. We sit in silence, bellies filled and bodies grateful for the fact we nearly lost each other today, but we did not.

After we all settle in for sleep, I wait for Abras. But when he comes, he just sits next to me with his legs curled up to his chest and his arms wrapped around them. I prop myself up on my elbows.

"What's wrong?" I whisper.

"I can't keep almost losing you."

"But you didn't. I'm here. We are both here." I try to reach for his arm, but he pulls it away.

"Yes, right now we are both here. But tomorrow? The next day? The world keeps pulling you from me, and I fear — one of these times — it will succeed."

"Abras, don't think like that. We've come so far. We arc so close."

"So close to what? Pru's farm where we don't even know if we will be welcomed or turned into the authorities? And then what? Some other force will just come along to rip us apart, to use our bodies for some new end."

"Abras, I don't understand. Where is this coming from?"

"I don't know. I just, I never expected anything, Cala. I never expected to be free. I never expected to love you. And I am. I do. But before, it was easier. Nothing could be taken from me because there was nothing to take. And now I have everything. You are everything. And I've almost lost you again, and it's too much."

"I could lose you, too. But we have to believe there's a possibility, a hope, that we won't. We have to fight for that. Because if we don't, we've lost each other already."

We both sit with our words for some time.

"Abras, this has been a lot these last few days. Too much. Just come lie here with me so you can feel my body, and you can know that right now, right here, you haven't lost me. I don't know what tomorrow will bring. At this rate, probably an earthquake and a pack of dirawolves."

"Or a swarm of cythas."

"Right." I smile into the darkness.

Abras lies down. I roll over so that I am facing away from him and scooch back into the space made by his body. He curls around me. I take his arm, pull it over me, and lace my fingers through his. Our hands rest by my heart.

"I love you, Abras. I would face an earthquake and a pack of dirawolves and a swarm of cythas for you."

"And I you," he says. "But I'd really prefer not to."

We both laugh softly. Eventually, the warmth of his body and the rhythm of his breath lull me to sleep.

***

Our plan is to wake early and take the forest route back north-westward toward Anterra. We want to be sure we are well beyond the town and anybody who might follow the declaration on the poster before we resume our trek on the trade road.

The rising sun is still low in the sky after a couple hours of hiking through the dark forest. We guess that we are a short way beyond the town, past the point where Sentaya and I turned around yesterday. In our exhaustion, we've been traveling in a drowsy, silent fog. Suddenly, Rayon, from his spot at the front of the line stops and puts his hand up for us to do the same.

"What's that sound?" he asks.

We turn our heads towards the steady sound coming from ahead in the forest, like a babbling whisper.

"Is that water?" Sentaya is the first to name it.

"The river!" shouts Rayon, and he is off running towards it. We have no choice but to follow.

As we approach, the whisper becomes a dull roar. A swift current ripples, eddying around rocks and branches sticking out of the water.

"It must be high from the recent rainfall," says Abras.

"How are we going to cross it?" asks Sentaya.

"I'm sure there's a bridge if we head back to the road," he replies.

"But are we far enough past the town to risk being seen?" I ask.

"I don't know," says Abras. "We'll have to take a risk with the townspeople or the water."

Not the water," says Sentaya. "It's too wide to jump across and too deep and fast to try wading. Plus, I don't know how to swim. Do any of you?"

We all shake our heads.

"Look down there," Rayon says. "There's a rock jutting out a bit from the bank on the far side." Our gazes follow his pointing finger.

"It's still too far to jump," says Sentaya.

"She's right," adds Abras. "Even my best leap would land me right in the middle of the river."

"I know," Rayon goes on. "But maybe it's far enough out that we could get to it with a log."

"What log?" Sentaya asks.

"Any log we can find. It's a forest."

We consider this for a moment as we examine Rayon's rock.

Soon, we are fanning out into the woods in search of the right log. After rejecting several logs on the basis that they were too decomposed to hold our weight, too heavy to carry, or too short to reach the rock, we finally settle on one.

Spreading out along the length of the log, we each try to get our arms around the thing.

"Ready?" says Rayon. "Lift."

The log is airborne. We stumble and sway and nearly lose footing at many points, but we manage to keep the log — and each other — from tumbling to the ground. Eventually, we make it to the shore and drop the log to plan our next move. There is much conversation about how to execute this part, landing the log securely on the rock.

Eventually, we decide that Rayon and Abras will wade as far into the river as they can holding the front of the log. Sentaya and I will guide the log from the back, slowly edging it forward while trying to hit our mark. Soon we have edged it forward enough that it bumps up against the rock.

We let out a collective, "Yeah!", as the log taps the rock from the rapids. But our cheers are quickly subdued when we realize how difficult it is to actually place the log onto the rock. Both are soaked, and despite the rock having a flat little groove on its edge, we can't seem to get the log to rest there. The strong pull of the current makes it impossible to hold the log steady enough to land it in the rock. And now our arms are starting to weaken from the effort of trying to fight the current.

"I'm not sure this will work," I say through labored breathing.

"Can you three hold this steady on your own?" Rayon asks.

"I think so," says Abras. "Why?"

Without answering, Rayon lunges himself into the river. Holding onto the log, he starts to pull himself across the river toward the rock.

"Rayon!" Sentaya and I gasp in unified horror. But all we can do is watch helplessly.

The current is so strong that it pulls his legs downriver, so he is gripping the log with his arms as his legs are swept out underneath him. The log still bobs and shifts as the current fights our grip on it. Slowly, hand over hand, he keeps propelling himself forward. I forget to breathe as I watch, waiting for him to lose his grip and get swept away by the current. His knuckles are white and his lips are taunt from the strain of it.

After what feels like hours but must only be minutes, Rayon reaches the rock. Near the opposite shore, the current is not quite as strong but still he fights to keep his grip. He must now let go of the log with one hand to reach for the rock. He extends his arm, grabs for the rock, but his hand slips, and for a moment the current unsteadies him and he tips backward, his head submerged underwater, but he is still gripping the log. From the opposite shore, the three of us roll the log forward to help pull him back up out of the water. He throws his body over the log, as he catches his breath then tries again.

For a moment he has one arm on the rock and one on the log, and he is jostled about as the log continues to ebb in the river. With effort, he launches his other arm up toward the rock, finds his grip, and kicks off of the log to push out of the water. He sprawls onto the rock and heaves for a few moments before flipping onto his back and shouting toward our general direction. "I'm all right!"

The three of us, exhausted from trying to hold the log steady and watching our brother nearly drown himself, simply stare at him incredulously from across the river.

By now he's sitting up and planning his next maneuver, pulling the log up onto the flat divot of the rock.

"Can you lift the log up so I can grab it and pull it up?" he shouts.

At this point, my arms are weak and shaking, and all I can think of is letting the beastly thing go.

But Abras rallies us, shouting back, "I think we can!"

Then he turns to us. "Let's get as far out as we can and then lift it up out of the water so Rayon can grab a hold. Ready?"

"I can barely keep holding it!" Sentaya says. "I'm not sure I can lift it up."

"We just need to do it for one more moment," I say, trying to convince myself as much as anyone. "We can do this."

So Sentaya and I wade out to Abras, and we all crouch down in preparation to lift the log up.

"On three," he says. "One-two-three!"

The three of us somehow heave the log up over our shoulders for just long enough before our strength gives out. Before I see it, I feel it. The log is steadied. It's no longer bobbing wildly in the current. Once Rayon has placed it on the rock, we are able to set our side down on the riverbank. We step back to give our aching arms a rest and to admire our bridge.

"Now what?" I say.

"Now, we cross and hope it holds," says Sentaya.

Sentaya prepares to go first, securing her pack on one side of her body and Rayon's on the other. We watch her sit astride the log, scooting her way across.

"Ouch!" she yells suddenly after making it about halfway across.

"Are you okay?" I call out from the bank.

"I snagged my leg on this branch sticking out. Be careful when you get to this spot."

After a moment, she continues scooting, but I notice she lifts her leg a bit, keeping it from rubbing against the log as she goes.

"I hope she's okay," I say to Abras, but my concern fades quickly as Sentaya reaches the rock and Rayon helps her scramble onto it. She jumps onto the opposite shore and whoops tiredly at reaching the other side.

"You're up!"' she calls back.

I follow Sentaya's lead, careful to lift my leg over the jutting branch where Sentaya snagged hers. Eventually, Rayon pulls me onto the rock then I leap into Sentaya's waiting arms on the shore.

"Is your leg okay?" I ask her.

"I think so," she says, reaching down to her right calf.

"All right, easy, Abras!" Rayon calls out as Abras begins scooting across the log.

"Almost there," I whisper.

Soon, he reaches the rock, and I exhale deeply, unaware that I had been holding my breath.

But my relief is premature. As Abras stands to take Rayon's hand, he loses his footing on the wet log. Their fingertips brush but can't connect. Abras's arms reach out but only find air, and he plummets backwards into the water. The speed of the river becomes visible as we watch Abras swept away by the current, a tiny speck upstream in mere moments.

I open my mouth to yell his name, but my chest seizes in panic, and no sound comes out. Some instinct takes over, and my legs are moving. We run, but the current is faster and carries him out of our sight.

I hear a voice behind me shout, "Cala! There! On the branch!"

It's Abras, clinging desperately to a partially submerged branch. I try to wade out to him, but it's too far.

Suddenly, Sentaya and Rayon come crashing into the water, carrying a thick branch between the two of them. All three of us grip it and extend it out towards Abras. He reaches for it with one, then both hands. Simultaneously, we pull the branch back toward the shore until we are all collapsing onto the bank in exhaustion. We lay, sprawled out and panting for some time.

"Are you okay?" I finally ask.

He breathes heavily for another moment before he responds. "You said earthquake, not river."

"Well, I suppose we'll just have to add it to the list." I pull him close to me and take in his body, whole and unbroken.

***

Once we are sufficiently dried, rested and fed, we resolve to continue further through the forest until we feel we have put enough distance between us and Anterra. Eventually, the road empties, and we feel safe enough continuing as we did before, listening for oncomers and taking refuge in the forest when needed.

I notice Sentaya putting her leg down a bit tenderly.

"Your leg," I say. "It's hurt. Here, sit. Let's look at it."

"I'm okay," she swats me away. "Let's just continue on. We have a lot of ground to cover before Galendale."

"Are you sure?"

"It's just a little sore from where I snagged it on that branch."

As the day wears on, remote farms and weather-worn homes begin to speckle the countryside, pockets of people trying to eke out a life for themselves. Whole families of children labor in the field alongside their parents. Girls — no older than ourselves — swollen with a child or with a baby on her hip. Children in tattered clothes, running shoeless in front of their houses, sometimes no parents in sight at all.

Sentaya pulls Father's leather pouch out and begins handing out coins to the children and saying, "Give this to your mamma." And the grubby, wide-eyed children take the precious coin as they watch us pass by.

The details change, but the landscape remains the same. Sometimes a stretch of farmland. Sometimes a cluster of small houses, too sparse to be considered a town. Once or twice a little town in its own right. But as we pass through the countryside of Arcalia, what doesn't change is that the people are poor and the women are run ragged. And by the time the sun goes down and we duck into the forest to set up camp, Sentaya's pouch is empty.

***

We've been lying around the fire for some time, each absorbed in our thoughts, when Sentaya finally speaks.

"I just keep thinking about all those children. They looked so hungry."

"And those women, sometimes barely women, with all those kids to look after and work to do. They seemed so…" I paused trying to find the right words. "So used up."

"They reminded me of the slaves back in the mine," Abras said. "They didn't seem any freer."

"How can a kingdom let its people live like that?" Rayon asks. How little he has seen of the world.

"People in power don't care about the rest of us," I say. "That's just the way of it, Rayon."

"It just seems so unfair," Sentaya says. "Those people need help beyond a coin from a passing stranger."

"That's what led Onaris to do what he did," Abras said. "Just helping people where he could, and then it became something more. The Servants did a lot of good in Urendia."

"These people need that kind of help," says Sentaya.

"The Servants just don't have that far a reach."

And suddenly the way forward becomes clear, as it did that day in the mine when I realized I held the fire powder that could bring it all down. Except this time, instead of destruction, it will be creation, sparks of light in dark places, of hope where none was there before.

"We will be The Servants of Arcalia," I say.

We stay up well into the night, caught up in our enthusiastic exchange about how we might go about becoming The Servants of Arcalia and all we would do. What we lack in experience and knowledge, we make up for in eagerness and sincerity. For now, that will have to do.

Chapter 12
Havita
Arcalia: Twenty Years Earlier

The whole village convened to mourn the loss of Perda's husband some months after our trek to the mountain peak. He has been a teria, like Akita, and had guided many members of the village toward tanouli over the years. People of many ages stood up to share what a gentle and patient guide he had been. I looked for Perda afterward, but she was nowhere to be found, more than likely halfway up the mountain by then.

On the path back toward the village clearing, Akita caught up to me.

"You've been progressing well since your time on the mountain, Havita."

"Thank you."

"I think you are ready for your yayuna, your time with nature."

"Haven't I been spending time with nature?"

He laughed. "This is different. You will spend three days in the wild."

"By myself?"

"Not by yourself. With your kimbasa."

"So I will spend three days in the wild with a herd of anterlope?"

"Precisely. You may stay longer than three days."

"If the anterlope extend the invitation?"

He laughed again.

"When will I leave for my yayuna?"

"Tomorrow. Perda has offered her supplies, and Haryana has prepared your food. You must leave before the sun is up."

He paused, and we walked in silence for a few strides.

"You are ready, Havita. Your heart is no longer clouded by anger. You will feel the connection with your kimbasa and the peace of tanouli."

***

Finding the herd of anterlope took only a matter of hours. By mid-morning, I was resting on my back in a meadow a short distance from where they grazed. Akita taught me that you know when you have connected with your kimbasa because they will accept you amongst their kind without fleeing or attacking. At least my kimbasa was the fleeing, and not attacking, type.

Up until now, I had only observed the anterlope from a distance. Akita had guided me to notice everything, from the newborn calves to the leader of the herd, the matriarch.

Despite the many variations of their hides, every one of them had a white diamond on their back. They moved nimbly and swiftly, whether they were dashing through the meadow or traversing the rocky terrain of the mountainside. Beyond being part of a large herd, there seem to be smaller social groupings among them.

During my training, Akita pushed me to focus on the leader, the female with the largest spiral horns. She grazed far less than her herd and only after the others were finished. She took a special interest in the young and seemed to remain close to the most fragile of the herd. It would be up to her to help her herd escape from a predator, such as the neru, mountain cat, or jula, wild dog. I had not observed the herd under attack, but I wanted to know how such a mild and graceful animal could possibly ward off a fierce predator.

The herd was on the move. So I got up to follow, trailing behind them all across the mountainside. The first day of my yayuna carried on in much the same way. I stayed to the outside, hesitant to spook the gentle creatures.

Come night, the anterlope settled in close to one another. I had the urge to lie among them, to feel the warmth of their bodies and to hear the cadence of their breathing. But instead, I lay alone on my mat inside my little makeshift tent, feeling a familiar loneliness settle in. And while the loneliness didn't stir my anger as it had before, it still left behind a longing. A longing to be held or sung to, for what my mother could not do for me so many years ago.

And so, I curled into a ball and wrapped my arms around myself in a hug. I gently sang the song that my father taught me when we sowed our new crop in the fields each spring.

> Little seed, small and firm,
> Take root amongst the soil.
> Make a friend with bug or worm,
> And then begin your toil.
> Little shoot, strong and green,
> Reach upward toward the sky,
> Don't give up and you'll be seen,
> By every human eye.
> Little plant, big and tall,
> Bear fruit and serve your end,
> You will feed, one and all,
> And become seed once again.

The anterlope stirred outside my tent, listening to my song. I waited to see if they would flee. But they soon settled. And so I sang my song again, feeling a little less lonely.

***

I woke to the heat of the late morning sun baking my tent. From my life on the farm to my pre-dawn kitchen duty at The Assassins' Guild to my morning lessons here on the mountain, it had been some time since I had woken up when I was ready and not when I had to. I stretched and basked in the luxury of it for a few moments when I remembered the anterlope. Surely the herd was long gone by now.

When I emerged from my tent, I was astounded to discover not only the entire herd still in the meadow, but the matriarch, standing nearby watching my tent. She eyed me intently for a few moments, then turned to head deeper into the mountain pass, the herd falling in line behind her. It was as much of an invitation as I was going to get.

I quickly packed up my camp and headed out, this time not trailing behind but in the thick of the herd, running to keep pace.

***

The matriarch led the herd with an urgency that I did not understand. When we passed a mountain lake, she stopped to water the herd only for a few brief moments before moving them along.

It was only as night fell that I understood her urgency. Off in the distance, the clouds darkened and fierce wind rattled the trees below. By then, she had led the herd through the valley of the mountain pass and into the thick protection of the pine forest. The herd grew restless as the temperature dropped and leaves and small twigs began to swirl chaotically into the air. They began to stomp and snort as raindrops fell, sporadically at first, and then suddenly in torrents.

But the matriarch stayed calm. She circled the herd, now gathered tightly in the forest, calming them as she passed by. She eyed me from time to time, and soon I began to follow her lead. I walked calmly through the herd, putting my hand on the diamonds of their backs, shushing them calmly to help them settle. She circled the exterior, and I moved through the interior of the herd, and even as the lightning illuminated their wide, panicked eyes and the thunder drowned out their stomping and snorting, the herd stayed in place and weathered the storm.

Late into the night, the storm abated, leaving behind a steady but gentle rain. The animals finally settled enough to lie down and sleep. By then, I was soaked and exhausted, and I laid in the center, welcoming the warmth of the many bodies around me.

***

I was jostled awake by the movement of the herd, rising to its feet and shaking off the remaining rainwater from their coats. The matriarch led them, with much less urgency this time, to a mountain lake and let them graze and drink leisurely for the morning.

I noticed she moved amongst them, seeming to check to see how they fared after the storm. Once again, I followed her lead and did the same.

It was then that I discovered a mother and her calf on the outskirts of the herd — the calf laid shaking on the ground while the mother hovered over him in concern. I had seen something similar on the farm, when animals had gotten caught out in cold weather. They would shake uncontrollably from the exposure, as if their body could not recover from the cold. The only way to help them was to warm them up by any means: fire, blankets, body heat. I was limited in what I could offer, but one thing there was no shortage of was body heat.

I gently nudged the mother, guiding her to lie down around her calf and helping her body wrap around his. Then I set to work guiding a few other anterlopes to the calf, and I positioned them around him as well, so that only his little head was exposed.

By now, the matriarch had made her way over, sniffing at the calf in concern. I lay down near the calf and cradled his head in my hands, trying to rub warmth back into it. We stayed like that for some time, and soon, the calf's violent shaking became more subtle and eventually, he was still and fell asleep in the warm tangle of bodies. I still cradled his head as he slept peacefully.

After a while, the matriarch came to where I laid and bowed low to me, holding the gesture for several moments.

Then, both our heads whipped simultaneously toward the edge of the clearing where a neru emerged from the forest.

***

The mountain cat stalked forward, and the anterlope herd sprang into action. The most developed among them with the strongest horns formed a defensive line, with the matriarch front and center. The rest of the herd fled behind us into the cover of the forest.

I pulled my knife from my belt and stood alongside the others. They began to make a sort of grunting sound as the neru approached, and I joined them. The matriarch glanced quickly behind to make sure the rest of the herd had fled to safety, then she led the charge toward the attacking cat.

The cat leapt swiftly toward us, and I was reminded instantly of Yera leaping at Sarrel those many months ago. He leapt over the advancing formation and landed behind us, forcing us to spin around, but not before the cat swiped at the backside of the male anterlope at my side. He went down, and we formed a line in front of him, blocking the cat from further attack.

The cat leapt again, but this time we understood his strategy. We rose our collective weapons in time to block him. Our defensive maneuver sent him tumbling off to the side, and we seized the opportunity to descend on him, coming at him with our horns (and my knife). The matriarch, with her strong, long horns, made contact first, piercing the side of the cat. He yelped and leapt away, skulking off into the forest from which he had come. The group divided, with the matriarch and me attending to the injured antelope and the rest rushing for protection in the forest.

As I knelt down beside the antelope, I saw that his injury was deep and his breathing slow. He looked fearfully into my eyes for a few desperate moments, and then he closed his eyes as his breathing stopped altogether. I fell over his battered, bloodied body and wept. After some time, the matriarch nuzzled me, and I slowly stood up to go.

***

Soon night fell upon the forest, and the herd huddled together to rest. It had felt like a harrowing day — the storm overnight and the neru attack today — but this was just the way of things for the antelope herd in these Tunic Mountains.

As I nestled into the herd for the evening, I thought about the relentless siege of danger issued from this world, and the constant need for protection. And I thought of the matriarch, ever vigilant, fiercely protecting every member of her herd from these ceaseless threats. It was the same instinct that my mother had, but she was crushed by the weight of it. I would not be.

The anterlope was my kimbasa. Not because I was weak or dashed off at the slightest sound, as I had once said to Yera. No, I was the anterlope because I was fierce, but also because I knew there was more to life than killing. There was loyalty. And kinship. And love. And those were things that were worth protecting, as the matriarch had shown me. So I would fight to protect those things in this world.

And sometimes I would fail and feel loss, like I had today, staring into the frightened eyes of the dying anterlope.

But sometimes I would succeed. And I would make the world better by protecting what was good in it. I drifted to sleep with a newfound understanding of my place in this world. A child of peace.

***

I returned to the village by the same path that led past Perda's dwelling. She was tending to chores busily as I approached. She stopped and turned to take me in.

"You have found tanouli," she said matter-of-factly, eyes glistening and mouth curved upward. "How do you feel?"

"I feel at peace."

"You look it." Then she added, "Well, aside from the dirt and blood coating every inch of you."

We both laughed. "I am happy for you, Havita."

"Thank you, Perda. Thank you for it all."

She bowed to me, as the matriarch had done, and then stood up and got back to her chores.

I continued down the path toward the village, eager to find Akita.

But I found someone very unexpected as I made my way through the tents. It was Yera who was waiting for me, eyes furrowed and hands wringing in worry.

"Havita, I bring word from your father. Your mother is sick. There is not much time. You must go now."

Chapter 13
Cala
Arcalia

I wake at some point in the night, our campsite still shrouded in darkness, to the sound of a moan.

"Abras?" I call.

He rolls over beside me. "It's not me."

"Rayon? Sentaya?" I call out.

"I'm fine," says Rayon groggily.

"Sentaya?" I call. But the only response is another moan.

We all crouch around Sentaya. Even after I gently nudge her shoulder, she doesn't open her eyes, just moans again. When I place my hand on her cheek to try to rouse her, her skin is hot.

"She's burning up!" I say, my hand on her forehead. "Is she sick?"

"Maybe," says Abras. "Didn't she cut her leg?"

"On the log. But she said it was okay. Why would that make her feverish?"

"If a wound gets infected, you get a fever. It happened in the mine. One of the slaves cut his arm on a pickaxe. After a few days, it was red and swollen and oozing yellow. Pru used an herb to help."

"What herb? Did it work?"

"I don't know, something from the yard, but I'm not even sure what it looks like." Abras looks away.

"Did it work?" I can feel the desperation rising in my chest.

"No, his body couldn't fight it. The infection was too bad by then. But Sentaya just got her cut yesterday, right? We just need to get help soon."

"But Galendale is still at least a day's journey from here, and that was with everyone walking. We'll have to carry Sentaya. It could take days!" My voice is rising with panic now.

Rayon is wide-eyed, looking from me to Abras and back to Sentaya.

Abras takes a steadying breath. "We're just going to have to stop at the next village we come to and get help."

"Yes, okay," I say, already stumbling around in the dark and starting to pack up camp. Abras and Rayon begin to do the same.

Then there is the matter of how to move Sentaya. We debate turning her bedroll into a sort of gurney, like the ones they'd use to carry the sick or dead out of the mine. But we don't have a frame to keep her body from dragging on the ground nor any kind of harness to be able to pull it. Abras suggests maybe she can walk assisted, and he and Rayon try to prop her up between

249

the two of them, but she just hangs limply and moans again. They lie her back down.

"We're just going to have to carry her," I say finally. Suddenly the image of Willa being carried back by three guards after trying to run away pops into my mind. A faint heartache for my friend stabs through the urgency of the situation for a moment before I'm pulled back by it.

"Abras, stand there at her legs. Rayon, you and I will each take an arm. We'll all face forward and walk with Abras at the lead."

We each crouch down next to Sentaya at our designated spots and hook our arms under her.

We lift her up, forming a triangle around her, pointed forward. Abras leads us back toward the road. The uneven forest floor in the cloud-covered night is difficult to navigate, and one of us loses our footing a couple of times, but eventually we make it out onto the road.

***

My time in the mine trained me in how to let my body take over during grueling work, leaving my brain free to wander. After an hour or two carrying Sentaya's left arm up the road toward an unknown destination, my arms begin to feel heavy and weak, and my back aches from the strain. My mind wanders away from the drudgery, and I find myself thinking about Mamma.

Would she proud of me? I think back to the shameful act of the letter, but then — the mine. If all went as planned, the mine will be nothing but rubble by now. And those who were once enslaved within it are safe and starting their lives anew. Surely, my mother committed a foolish deed or a selfish act along the way. Is the best we can do to hope that, when all is counted and settled, our good acts outnumber our bad?

"Look. Up ahead." Abras points to a figure, materializing where the road meets the horizon.

"Do we take cover?" Rayon asks.

"I think we need to ask how far the next village is," I say.

"I agree," says Abras. "If it's much further, we may need to adjust our strategy."

My tired arms tremble in agreement. So, we continue toward the approaching traveler.

Soon, we halt in front of a man in a wagon and a brown horse. We set Sentaya down on the side of the road to give our arms a rest. She moans but doesn't rouse.

He tips his cap and calls down from the wagon seat, "Hello there."

"Might you know how far until the next village?"

"About an hour at Jessa here's pace." He leans down and pats his horse on the neck. "Couple more for you folks, as I see it. You in some kind of trouble?" He nods towards Sentaya lying off to the side.

"My sister is sick," I say. "Do you happen to know if the village had a doctor?"

"Can't say. I was just passing through and had no need to ask after a doctor, as fortune would have it."

"We'd better keep moving then," I say.

He looks over to Sentaya and back to us. "Listen, I happen to find myself ahead of schedule today. Why don't you all get in the wagon and Jessa and I will take you back toward the village, won't we, girl?" He leans down to pat his horse again.

The three of us look at each other, uncertain. Sentaya needs help fast, and our arms are just about through. But we don't know if this man can be trusted.

"Besides," he goes on. "Haven't done my one good thing today."

"Your one good thing?" Rayon asks.

"Yeah, got to do one good thing each and every day. Some days on the road, I don't pass a single soul, so my one good thing is extra brushes for Jessa. Isn't that right, girl?"

He pats her again, and this time she whinnies in response.

"We would be most thankful," I say. And the others nod in agreement. We load Sentaya gently into the wagon and climb in behind her.

As the man leads his horse around to face the opposite direction, he tilts his head our way. "Halander Druvel, at your service."

The relief of being seated and empty-armed begins to spread through my aching body. We take the opportunity to eat a bit and drink some water. I try to give Sentaya some water again, and this time she takes a bit down, a good sign. Rayon curls up on the wagon floor like a cat and is snoring in what seems like an impossibly short amount of time. Abras and I manage a smile at each other. I rest my head on his shoulder. He takes my hand and kisses it.

"It's going to be okay, Cala. She's going to be okay." I kiss his hand back before dozing until I'm jolted awake by the wagon coming to a stop.

***

As Halander Druvel disappears down the road — having done his one good thing today — we turn towards the village, not much more than a few crumbling wooden buildings with faded thatched roofs.

Abras nods towards a door about halfway down the way. "How about that one? Looks like a tavern, maybe."

"You go in," I say. "Rayon and I will stay here with Sentaya."

We settle Sentaya in front of a tree, and Rayon and I take up post on either side of her as we watch Abras disappear into the tavern. We've spent the entirety of our journey avoiding people whenever possible. To sit here so clearly exposed and to know that Abras is inside an unknown establishment leaves me spinning. But

Sentaya's life hangs in the balance, and we have no choice. I stroke her hair to calm her as much as myself.

"They don't have a doctor," Abras tells us when he returns. "But there's a midwife. A ways off the main road. I have directions."

Abras reaches down, offering Rayon and me each an arm. He pulls us onto our feet, and then we go about lifting Sentaya back into the triangle formation.

"There's a small dust path up ahead," says Abras. "We take that until we see a bera tree with a split trunk. Then we follow that path until we reach her house, a small cottage tucked back into the woods."

And so we carry on, our bodies taking over once again as we grow warm and tired under the midday spring sunshine.

"There, a split trunk. Is that it?" Rayon asks after some time.

"That's a bera tree, I think. The innkeep said we'd recognize it by its white bark."

We turn onto the small path, barely visible from the overgrown branches and bushes. Soon a small, stone cottage emerges, half covered in moss and vines. A large woman is out front in a garden bigger than the house, several children working alongside her.

"Excuse me!" I call out. She looks up at us. The children freeze.

"We are sorry to bother you," I begin again. "The innkeep in town told us where we could find you."

She stands all the way up now — her sturdy frame taking shape before us — as her four young children line up beside her.

"We don't want any trouble," I say. "My sister is sick with fever. We were hoping you could help."

She speaks now for the first time. "What kind of fever?"

"She cut her leg. We think it's from that."

"How long ago?"

"About a day and half."

"Can you pay?"

"A little," I say, thinking of the few coins we have left for our stay in Galendale.

She pauses for another moment, taking us in.

"No guarantees," she says, turning toward the house. She disappears inside, leaving us unsure of what to do.

"She means for you to follow." A soft-spoken little girl translates for us. The pack of children turn to go inside, and so do we.

In the corner of the one-room, dimly lit cottage, the woman is stripping a bed with such vigor it seems she might tear the sheets.

"Clean sheets! Boiled water! Fresh bandages!" she calls out to no one in particular, but this sends the children scampering in different directions.

She waves us over and motions for us to lay Sentaya on this freshly made bed.

"Where's the wound?"

"Here, on her right leg," I say, starting to roll up her pant leg.

"Leave it," she says. "Your dirty hands will only make it worse."

I pull back my hands, suddenly aware of the dirt-stained skin and mud-caked fingernails.

By now her children are beginning to bring the rest of the supplies. She scrubs her hands unflinchingly in a bowl of scalding water then takes a strip of cloth, dips it into another bowl of water, and begins to dab at Sentaya's now exposed leg. Sentaya moans.

"Shhh, there, there," she says with a hint of gentleness that was undetectable before.

Not lifting her eyes from her work, she begins to give directions. "I'll need a poultice for the wound. Most of it can be found in the garden and forest. But we need to go into town for dried timeran root. It's the best thing to help her fight this infection. Dera will take one of you into the woods to find the plants for the poultice. Creya will take you into town. You have to know where to go. You." She points to me.

"Cala," I say.

"Cala, you stay here with your sister. We need her to remain calm."

Rayon goes with Dera into the woods for the varied plants and roots needed for the poultice, while Abras and Creya head back into town. I feel pulled in three directions and wish I could somehow stay with each of them.

The midwife must sense my worry. "They're in good hands."

I nod, gratefully. "I'm so sorry. I didn't get your name."

"I didn't give it to you," she says, matter-of-factly. "It's Berta."

I settle onto the stool beside the bed, stroking Sentaya's hand, as Berta continues to work. She cleans the wound and places a cool linen on Sentaya's forehead. Her smaller children begin to return from the garden with various leaves and roots, which Berta puts into a stone mortar and begins to grind.

"I picked the baby shoots from the sepra leaves, Mamma," the little girl says.

"Good girl." Berta smiles warmly at her daughter. "Mita, could you put the kettle on? Cala, here, looks like she could use some tea."

The little girl turns toward the wood stove.

"We'll need to wait for the rest of the ingredients," says Berta, eyes still on Sentaya's wound. "This won't be enough to fight the infection."

We sit in an awkward silence for a stretch. Berta wrings her hands; I can tell that this is a woman who is not used to sitting idly.

Soon our mugs of tea arrive, and I let the warmth of it settle me.

"Do you…" I begin, looking around. "Is it just you and your children here?"

"Are you asking after my husband? He went off some years ago to serve in the king's guard. Sent money back and came home to us every leave at first. But as the years passed, the money and the visits became fewer and further between until they stopped altogether."

"I'm sorry." It is all I can think to say.

"I'm not. My mamma trained me in the ways of healing as did hers before that. Me and my girls got all we need right here. Townsfolk find their way here when they need this or that. It's enough for us to get by."

I marvel at her self-reliance. To live a life entirely unreliant on a man seems almost impossible to me. Even Teetee, who was more defiant than I had known, could not escape the confines of a man's world, being passed from her father to my father, and ultimately over to the authorities. But here's a woman who lives only for herself and her daughters. A yearning for this kind of freedom stirs inside me.

Soon the door opens, and Rayon and Dera return with a basketful of plants, roots and barks.

"It's too early for hessa blooms, but I found some dried moss instead."

"That will do," Berta says, taking the basket. "That will do fine. As soon as we have the remaining ingredients, we will do our best to bring that fever down."

Rayon and Dera settle in nearby with their own mugs of tea. The warmth of the tea and the dimness of the room lull us into a stillness that causes me to notice how very tired I am, a tired that reaches all the way to my bones.

Suddenly the door bangs open, the wood crashing into the stone wall. Creya stoops over, hands on thighs, drawing deep breaths.

Finally, she says between breaths, "They said Abras was a wanted fugitive. They took him. They're coming for the rest of you. They're nearly here."

Chapter 14
Havita
Arcalia: Twenty Years Earlier

When I finally walked back up that old worn stone path to our front door, taking in my home for the first time in some years, I saw a silhouette in the window, a seated figure facing eastward.

"Mamma," I whispered.

But as I got closer, I saw that the figure was too tall and the head too round. It was my father who kept vigil at the window. And I understood from the pained look on his face. I was too late.

***

I wanted so much to turn around, to go back to the herd of anterlope and nestle among them, fierce protector of a simpler world. It was only the pained look on my father's face, the same one he had the day I left, that drew my feet forward. I could not leave him again. Not now.

So, I walked into my home, where he was now waiting for me, arms outstretched. I fell into those arms, and we collapsed together onto the floor. I cannot say how long we stayed that way, holding each other and sobbing great heaving sobs, when finally he drew a deep breath and said, "She wanted me to give you something." He disappeared into the other room briefly and came back, holding a letter.

***

My Dearest Elina,

I write these words as I prepare to leave this world, which is a relief in almost every way, save one: I will not get to hold my daughters again.

That I did not hold you every day, that I did not make you feel cherished, is my greatest regret. They took Pru from me, that I could not control, but you I could have had, and yet, I let you go too. I wish with my whole heart that I could go back and shake myself from my grief and my fear, casting off its shadow that made me lose my way. But instead, I stumbled blindly through it, and the only way out was to keep you safe. I broke you to save you, because I could not save Pru.

Please, my darling, please understand that it was all from love. That is not an excuse; I would not dare defend what I have done. But I hope that it offers you at least some comfort. I loved you even when you were a tiny thing inside me. My love for you was greater than the impossibility of losing another child. Every day that I dumped that thustle tea back into the earth was a triumph of my love for you. I wish my love had triumphed in greater ways in the years since, but alas, I am a broken woman, too.

I am so very sorry, my beautiful girl. I loved you from the very first. I loved you every moment since. I love you now as I prepare to leave this world. And I am certain I will love you hereafter. Please, my love, find peace. Nothing is ever broken beyond repair.

Yours most devoted,

Mamma

Much later, this letter would bring me peace. It would be read countless times throughout my life. It would take on new meaning as I grew. It would keep me tethered to my mother, not the mother who sent me off as a child, but the mother who loved me, who wanted so desperately to protect me, who was what I needed.

But in that moment, the grief of hearing my mother's words — no of reading them and knowing I would never hear them again — was unbearable. The pain in my chest threatened to rip me apart. I wished it would.

My father held me and rocked me as I sobbed on the floor. As I screamed, "Why did she leave me again?" over and over until my voice was raw. And then, he put me in my bed, where I collapsed, utterly spent, weighed down by the agony of knowing that she had never held me, and now, she never would.

For the first time in almost two years, I awoke in my bed to the familiar sounds of our farm. The animals flocked as their feed troughs were filled and Cuppa the horse whinnied as she was hooked up to the plow and the farmhands called to one another as the day got under way. It was early fall, which meant harvest season, and no force in the world, not even the death of my mother, could stop the busyness of harvest season. Our entire year's livelihood, as well as those we employed, depended on a successful harvest.

So, I pulled myself from my bed and my grief, got dressed, and got to work.

I found my father in the barn, stacking crates of grain.

"Where are the cows?"

"I sold 'em after you left. Just didn't have enough help to keep up with the milking with you gone and your mother sick."

"I'm sorry, Pappa."

"You don't be sorry. You don't ever be sorry. To know that you carry that on top of everything else... your mother wouldn't have wanted it."

My chest tightened at the mention of her. I wasn't ready to talk about this.

"Well, I'm here now. Where do you need me?"

And with that, I picked right back up as if I had never left. My father had me work with Cuppa on the plow. It was good, hard work requiring my full attention, which I gratefully took up.

Work on the farm starts at first light and goes until the moon is up at harvest time. There is little else to do but work. The familiarity of it was a comfort, and the grueling hours were a distraction. That is how I made it through those first weeks.

It was only in the evenings, when my father and I settled into the quiet house, that I had to confront my grief. And then, it was my father who got me through it.

At first, we talked about nothing of great consequence. The details of the harvest, or news from the village since I left, or even sometimes, old stories from my childhood, like when I insisted on sleeping in the barn because I was convinced I would wake up a cow.

As time went on, we began to slowly creep into weightier topics. My father started to ask about my time away. And I told him of The Assassins' Guild and of their motto and of how I tried so desperately to live it. I told him of the friendships I formed with Yera and Auntie Cook and even Trina, in her own way. And then, ultimately of the night when I confronted my true identity, and I saved a life instead of ending one.

Later, I told him of my time on the mountain and how Perda helped me let go of my anger.

My father listened to my stories, taking in each detail with unblinking attention. When he understood that the training my mother had subjected me to — that he had allowed — hadn't stamped out my true nature, he put his head down and wept.

Finally, he picked his head up. "I was so afraid we destroyed you. What a strong woman you are, Elina."

"Do you think… would you call me 'Havita'?"

He considered this a moment. I tried to read his face, but I could not determine whether it was pride or pain I saw there. Maybe both.

"Yes, of course," he said.

After some time, I began to ask about my mother. Sometimes, it became too difficult for one or both of us, so he told her story in pieces. But eventually, I understood what had happened in the nearly two years since I left.

"The truth of it," he said one night, staring into the fireplace as we both held out our hands for warmth, "is that she was impossible. After you left, I couldn't get her out of bed, and it was just like when Pru left. But then, when she started to get sick and the doctor came and said he didn't think she had long, I couldn't get her to stay in bed."

"Where did she go?"

"I don't know. She'd slip out while I was sleeping, out in her nightgown in the black of night!" he exclaimed, still clearly exasperated by it. "But then, slowly, she began to change. When she came home from her wanderings, she started talking to me, not the frantic worry or the wailing despair from when she couldn't leave the bed. She started to tell the story of her life, or at least her motherhood, but now with a new clarity. It was as if she had been in there all along, trapped beneath a veil of fear and anguish, and now for the first time, she had cast it off."

"Maybe it was the moon bath," I said, smiling as I thought of Perda.

"The moon bath?"

"Bathing in the light of the moon. The Tunic Mountain people believe it can awaken what lies dormant within. Maybe as Mamma wandered those nights, the moonlight awakened her clarity about everything."

"If I had known that was all it took, I would have tossed her out in the full moon years ago." Our laughter broke apart the sadness a bit, scattering it about the room.

"I might have thrown you both out for good measure," I added. And we laughed again.

But soon the sadness pieced itself back together and settled around us once more. "As the end drew near, I think the clarity was more painful than the veil of fear and anguish. She understood all too well what she had done and that she'd never be able to repair it. I wanted so much to give her the chance, but there was nothing I could do. I felt so helpless as I watched her struggle with it."

"I should have been here," I said through tears. "I should have given her the chance."

"That's the impossibility of it all, Elin... Havita. Your mother wanted so desperately to repair what she had done, but you had to leave here to repair it. You had to find tanouli and learn from your kimbasa. Staying here wouldn't have saved you, and in the end, that is what your mother wanted."

I was sobbing now. "But why did she have to die on top of it? Why couldn't I have said goodbye?"

He moved closer to me, holding my hand to his tear-streaked lips. "I don't know, my flower, I don't know." It was the nickname he called me when I was a child, and the warmth and familiarity of it wrapped around me like a blanket.

"As the time got near, she wrote and rewrote that letter to you until she was satisfied. She held it to her chest as she left this world. Your name escaping her lips was her last breath."

***

Soon, the busyness of the harvest season was over, and the sudden stillness of winter descended upon the farm. I found myself wandering through the meadow and up onto the mountain, wondering if maybe I was walking the same path that Mamma had walked at the end.

One winter afternoon, when the snow glistened in the sunlight and the beauty of it made you forget your frozen fingers and toes, I found my way to the empty barn. I ran my fingers over the wooden stalls where I had spent many such frozen afternoons tending to the cows, who were now all sold off.

The barn had always been my refuge when my mother's sullenness made the air in the house unbreathable. I would curl in the warm hay and talk to the cows, imagining what they might say in response. Oftentimes, I would fall asleep, and my father would come find me and carry me to my bed.

I thought then about how I no longer needed protection — not from the dangers of the world and not from the sullenness of my mother. Now, instead, I felt a fierce need to protect others, to settle the frightened herd as the storm raged on. This barn, now sitting empty, had been a source of protection. And suddenly, I understood that it would be again.

***

"Too far," I called up to my father as he clung to a ladder with one arm, reaching up with the other to hang a wooden sign. "A little further back the other way."

"Here?" he called down, holding the sign carefully over the barn doors.

"Perfect!" I shouted back up, and he began hammering it in place.

When the snow melted for good after my first winter back, my father and I set to work fixing up the barn. We would put in a few hours when we could amidst the planting, growing, and harvesting that year.

We painted the barn with a fresh coat of auburn. We tore down the stalls and patched some rotted wood and swept and swept and swept. And now, in the last days of the harvest, this sign was the final piece. I took a few steps back to take in, reading the perfectly carved letters that spelled out 'Pru's Place'.

After, he carefully climbed down the ladder, one slow step at a time, and I saw that he was no longer the strong, young man he had been my whole childhood.

"Just got back from the Hadera farm," I said. "They'll send their girls when they're done with their last work of the season."

"That makes twelve," my father said, taking in the sign. "Not bad for your first class."

I had spent the better part of the last year talking with neighbors about sending their girls to Pru's Place during the winter season, when they weren't needed on their farms. It was not easy convincing them. "What would they learn?" they all wanted to know.

They would learn to protect themselves.

Many, mostly fathers, sent me away, saying their daughters had all the protection they needed.

But some understood the need for protection. Many of the parents of these children had been siblings — the ones left behind — during The Offering. They saw what could happen in this world when you could not protect yourself. They saw what happened to their parents when they could not protect their own children.

Others had been the unsuspecting victims of tax collectors or local officials, seeing something they liked and taking it with impunity.

And others still knew that their girls could be victim to a quick hand or a swift kick without ever leaving their homes. That sometimes, the greatest threat came from those who were supposed to protect you.

So some families, after looking around to be sure no one saw, welcomed me in to talk more.

And then the next question was always about cost.

Which was nothing.

And in turn, the girls would learn how to handle a weapon and how to defend themselves using only their bodies. They would learn how to use herbs, to heal and to harm. They would learn the ways of tanouli so that they could harness their true nature to protect themselves and find peace in their hearts. And finally, they would learn to read and write because my mother, through her brokenness, had taught me that an educated woman is a powerful woman.

***

On that first day, when the twelve girls sat on the cold barn floor, looking up at me expectantly, I waited for the uncertainty to set in. But it didn't. I was a protector, and finally, I was living out my nature. I felt at peace.

We fumbled our way through an education. Most of the girls had never had any learning of any kind, so they struggled with the parts that required them to be still and focused, such as learning their letters or the purposes of various plants. They were farm girls and used to the activity of farm chores.

I learned to go slow and start where they were. At first, they could only sit and learn for a short while, and then we would get up and throw knives or mix dried herbs or hike into the mountains.

Many had been taught not to use their voices, not to question or offer an opinion. It was hard to break them of that, to teach them that their voice mattered. But when they finally started to talk, I learned that they had rich inner lives. And even though they hadn't expressed it, they *had* learned to question and form opinions. Once they knew that someone was interested in hearing them, there was no quieting them.

Some days, we lost entire lessons to the discussions that erupted in that cold barn as we sorted seeds or sharpened knives. But soon, I learned that this was part of the education, and no loss at all.

As the ground thawed and the girls were needed back home, we had our final lesson, and the they walked home for the last time. And while it was hard to let them go, to say goodbye yet again, I took heart in watching them walk away that spring, standing taller and surer than they had before.

***

Over the years, Pru's Place protected many Arcalians in a great many ways. As the winters wore on, the girls and women from neighboring farms and villages came to learn. And soon, word got around that ours was a place where someone could come when they needed help. We housed mothers and their children needing a safe place to stay. We gave parents food to take home to their families when they could not do so themselves. And when we could, we gave those parents work on the farm so as to give them their dignity too. And on occasion, we opened the door in the dark of night to find a young woman asking simply for 'the deed'.

We did not have much to spare, but we gave what little we could. And in return, folks helped in ways that they were able. A carpenter from the next village over helped us patch our leaky roof one spring when the rains did not stop for days. He said that his daughter — now a young woman — had been able to defend herself when an attacker tried to take her coin purse. One harvest when the fever struck our farm and many of our farmhands fell ill, nearby families sent a family member or two so that we didn't lose our harvest. And as my father began to move a bit slower and eventually could not move at all, the doctor came, free of charge, because his daughter, now his assistant, helped him save a great many more lives with the knowledge of herbal remedies she had learned at Pru's Place.

One summer evening, the doctor leaned over with his head on my father's chest, listening to his heart.

"It's weakening, I'm afraid," he said to me with his head still gently on my father's chest. "There is nothing to do."

After the doctor left that night, I knelt beside his bed, holding his hand between mine, staring tearfully at my father's sleeping face. I felt my eyes darting from feature to feature, filled with a sudden urgency to remember every line, every curve, every wrinkle even.

With eyes still closed, my father spoke gently to me.

"I am a lucky man, Havita. I saw you grow into a beautiful woman. I saw your broken heart repaired. Part of me left with Pru that day so many years ago, but what is left of me is at peace, because of you."

His lips slowly turned upwards into a smile, as if convincing me.

"Now, I will see your mother in the beyond, and I will tell her that your heart is no longer broken. And then, hers will be whole, too."

"But I don't want to be without you. I don't want to be alone." I dropped my head onto his hand, which he had opened to cradle it. He stroked my forehead with his thumb.

"It is a great sadness to leave you, Havita. These years with you, and the many people that have come to us for protection, these have been the happiest years of my life. You have given me such a gift."

I sobbed into his palm and he stroked my forehead until we both fell asleep. When I awoke in the night, he was gone. The candle on the windowsill — nearly burned to the end — cast a dim light across my father's face, mouth still turned upward in a smile.

I picked up what remained of the candle and found my cloak. The moonlight guided me as I made my way to the mountaintop to cry into the wind, this time, not in anger, but grief.

***

In the years since my father's death, I have carried on. With much hired help, I have been able to run the farm and turn enough profit to serve the people of Arcalia in any way that I can. Somehow, I have been running Pru's Place for over twenty years and have had over two hundred students. My first students, mothers now, have raised their daughters with the teachings I instilled in them. It occurs to me often that, had I stayed in The Assassins' Guild, instead of teaching some two hundred girls to protect themselves, I could have murdered that many people.

One spring afternoon, I sit in the chair that my mother kept vigil in all those years ago, facing eastward down our stone path. The spring breeze blows through the newly green leaves, casting dancing shadows on the path. Suddenly my eyes are drawn to three figures turning onto the path from the dusty road. As they come closer, I can see that they are not much older than children, two of them supporting the third, a girl, between them.

I rise from the chair to greet them, opening the door before they knock. Many a weary traveler has come to my door in search of help over the years, bringing with them countless stories — tragic, harrowing, seemingly impossible stories. But none of those stories shocked me the way these words do.

"Hello, I am Cala. I believe you may have known our grandmother, Pru."

Chapter 15
Cala

The woman looks down at me from her doorstep, but I cannot read her expression. She is middle aged, with short, sandy colored hair peeking out from behind a scarf that she wears on her head. At first, it doesn't seem she will answer at all, and I realize that it may have been a mistake to mention our names — Cala and Pru — both of us wanted fugitives.

But then—piercing down at me from a face etched with wrinkles and scars—are tearful, pale blue eyes. And I knew those eyes. They are Granna's. And they are my own.

"Yes," she says finally. "Pru was my sister. I suppose that makes me your great-aunt."

She steps down onto the front stoop and pulls the three of us into a tight hug. The fear and worry that I have fought down since we left the midwife's cottage, since we lost Abras, comes flooding to the surface, and I collapse into this woman — my great-aunt — and sob.

***

Somehow, she bears the weight of us as we hug for some time, then ushers us inside and seats each of us around her kitchen table, busying herself preparing tea. By now — thanks to the poultice that the midwife hurriedly mixed and sent with us as we fled her house — Sentaya's fever has broken and she is alert. Rayon still seems bewildered and shocked from the journey from the midwife's cottage, where we hid in the forest while Sentaya healed enough.

Once she has given us all a mug of tea and some bread with jam, she sits down at the table and says, "Now then, start at the beginning."

As difficult as it is to muster the strength, I do. Not at the beginning of my story, of course, but the beginning of Granna's. I tell my aunt — Havita, she told us — what happened to Pru once she was taken. Of her son, our father, and what he became. Of our journey here, and Rayon and Sentaya jump in to add their own perspectives or simply to carry on when I need to collect myself. I tell her of my time in the mine and of Granna and Abras and all The Servants. And then, I get to the escape plan, and what happened when we fled the mine into Arcalia. Rayon has to take over when I get to the part at the midwife's cottage and Abras's abduction.

It is almost evening, and by now, I am spent. But Aunt Havita makes us retell her everything about Abras's abduction. We tell her what little we can: the approximate location and size of the village. The few details the midwife's daughter told us about the

277

authorities who took him; it was the constable of the village, who arrested him based on a poster that was circulating. He had told her, "You best run off before I call in the king's guards, and then you will really be in trouble!"

"So it was just the one constable, and he had not called in any reinforcements when you left," she repeats back. "How many days ago?"

"It was the day before yesterday, in the afternoon," I say.

"If he sent word to the nearest fort, it would likely be Revinya, which is a day's ride by horse. If they sent guards back immediately, that's two days. We still have time, but I'll need to leave tonight if we stand a chance."

"I'm coming with you," I say, although simply uttering the words takes considerable effort.

"I admire your spirit, Cala, but we have the best chance of getting Abras back if I go alone. I will need to ride at full speed. And you need your rest."

"Thank you."

"Do not thank me yet. A long ride and quite a bit of luck stands between us and the rescue. You will find beds in the loft. I will be back as quickly as I can."

I feel hope stir faintly, but the exhaustion is too heavy for it to flourish into anything more.

***

The next morning, I awaken to a quiet house and the realization that Aunt Havita has not returned. I climb down the ladder from the loft and find Sentaya sitting in the kitchen with a mug of tea.

"She is not back," I say, sitting beside her at the table.

"Take heart in that, Cala. She said it would be most of a day's ride at full speed. If she were back, it would mean she didn't make it to Abras."

"You're right. But the waiting is unbearable."

She offers me a mug of tea and a smile.

"Where is Rayon?" I ask.

"Exploring," she says.

"Of course he is." I smile despite the worry that has taken residence in my stomach. My smile fades as a thought nestles in my mind. Suddenly, it occurs to me that she may not make it back either. From the looks of it, she is a middle-aged woman running a farm. Will she even stand a chance against whoever is holding Abras?

Just then, Rayon comes flying in through the door. "Sentaya, Cala! I think you should come see this."

We follow Rayon to a large barn set a ways back behind the house. I am startled to see a faded wooden sign over the door. Sentaya sees me taking it in.

"What does it say?" she asks.

"Pru's Place," I gasp.

"There's more," says Rayon waving us inside. He pulls back the big barn door to reveal, well, not a barn at all. Inside, there are makeshift walls creating different spaces. One has desks, shelves with books and paper. Another has many dried plants hanging from the rafters and countless bottles of what appears to be crushed leaves, barks and flowers. Another space has every type of weapon you could imagine displayed neatly on a wall: throwing knives, an axe, even a crossbow.

"Well, I guess she's not just a middle-aged woman running a farm," Sentaya says eventually.

"What is this place?" I ask.

"It looks like some kind of school," says Rayon. "Or training room."

"I think you're right," says Sentaya.

"Aunt Havita must be some kind of teacher," says Rayon. "I wish my schooling had been a little more like this. Then maybe I would have paid attention."

Sentaya and I laugh, but Rayon does not. I realize that his childhood has left its own kind of scars.

***

We spend the rest of the day wandering around the farm, trying to reconcile what we are seeing with the stories that Pru told me. I imagine her walking barefoot through this meadow, and it makes me sad, both because I miss her terribly and because it is so painful to see the life that was stolen from her.

Soon, evening comes but without Aunt Havita. We poke around in her kitchen and find some smoked fish and bread for dinner. We sit around the table amidst spurts of subdued conversation until the candle burns out.

"Well, shall we go up to bed?" Rayon asks.

"You two go," I say. "I'm going to wait up a bit longer."

They rise to go. Sentaya kisses me on the head as she walks past. I realize — despite the uncertainty of Abras's rescue and the unknown whereabouts of Teetee and Gran — what a gift it is to be here, safe on Pru's farm with my siblings. It amazes me that even amidst the most precarious of circumstances, there is joy to be found.

I sit awake in the dark for some time, thinking of Granna moving about this kitchen and sitting in this very chair. Eventually, I lay my head down on my arms and fall into a fitful sleep.

Chapter 16
Havita

I have journeyed many hours of the night, desperate to reach the village, and Abras, before the guards of Revinya do.

I have known these people mere hours, and yet, I take on their ordeal as if it were my own. But they are my family, the first family I have known in many years. How can I not protect them — and their friends — with this measure of fierceness?

As dawn makes her honey gold announcement, the silhouette of the village I believe Cala described appears. I slow Cuppa to form a plan. If the guards have not yet arrived, and I pray they haven't, it will likely be me against the constable. It is not the match-up that worries me — he is likely some bloated official given a position of status based on a connection or some other undeserved reason — but the prospect of Abras getting hurt in the crossfire. People are unpredictable when outmatched, and I am not sure how this constable will react. I decide the element of surprise is the best approach. Perhaps I can extract Abras without even involving the constable.

I locate what appears to be a tavern and slip inside. I stride toward the barkeep. "I've spotted some fugitives on the outskirts of town and would like to report them to the constable. Where can I find him, if you please?"

The barkeep eyes me for a harrowing moment before replying, "Last house on the left."

The last house on the left is a dilapidated wooden structure, with a sagging front porch and boarded up windows. It seems the constable is not a particular sort of fellow, which I can only see working out to my advantage. To my disadvantage, however, is the fact that I have no way of seeing into the house on account of the boarded up windows.

That is when I spy a hole in the roof. Typical.

I put one testing foot onto the sagging porch before stepping onto what's left of the railing and pulling myself silently up onto the roof. I creep toward where I spied the hole, pausing when the roof squeaks in complaint beneath me, until I reach it. I slide down onto my belly and peer in. The interior is as rundown as the rest of the house: papers littering the desk, burned candles scattered on the floor, plates of half-eaten food on every surface. The constable is in the center of the mess, cheek smooshed against a desk, snoring loudly. Amidst the cluttered desk I spy a brown jug, which accounts for his loud snoring.

The back of the dwelling has a wall of bars, and behind them, a young, brown-haired man staring directly at me.

"Hello," I whisper.

"No need to whisper," he calls back, startling me. "I don't suppose he'll be stirring anytime soon."

I glance back toward the constable, whose snoring only seems to grow louder.

"Well, are you friend or foe?" the prisoner calls again.

"That depends. Are you Abras?"

"That's me."

"Friend, then." I call back. "Let's see about getting you out of here."

Chapter 17
Cala

I am pulled from sleep by a whisper in my ear. "Cala."

I jolt awake and try to take in my surroundings, but it is pitch black.

"Cala, it's me."

And with those words, I know exactly where I am. I am home.

"Abras!" I wrap my arms around him. "You're okay," I exhale.

He hugs me back until I can't breathe, and soon I hear Rayon and Sentaya scampering down the ladder. Within moments, they are wrapped around us, too. I glance at Aunt Havita, who has lit a lantern by now, taking in the scene from the doorway with a grin on her face.

"How did you manage it?" I ask eventually, once we are all seated around the table, Aunt Havita and Abras ravenously eating.

"I wish I could report a more daring rescue mission," says Aunt Havita in between bites. "But it seems the constable responsible for taking in Abras is a bit of a drunk."

Abras laughs. "That's putting it mildly. The jailhouse is a one-room building, with a tiny cell in the corner of the constable's living quarters. So, I got to watch as he bumbled about, drinking ale and shouting at me about what was coming my way when the guards arrived. But he passed out at his desk in the middle of writing the letter. He was out for the rest of that first day and into the next, so when he finally came to and remembered what he was doing, a whole day had passed."

"By the time I arrived," Aunt Havita says, "the guards were nowhere near the village, and the constable was well into another stupor. Slipping in and rendering him unconscious was hardly necessary. I did it anyway, of course, but he was halfway there on his own. Hardly the stuff of heroes' tales."

"Well, heroes' tales or not," Abras says. "I was most grateful to be rescued." He tips his head at Aunt Havita, and she bows slightly back to him.

"Speaking of heroes' tales," says Rayon. "What in this world do you do in that barn!"

Aunt Havita laughs. "Perhaps it's time I told you my story."

***

We spend only a few days resting and regaining our strength because it is springtime, and the farm is a busy place. When we feel able, we begin to pitch in. It is hard work, but we relish being in the fresh air and sunshine, another world from the labor in the suffocating mines. And it is a different thing altogether, laboring on your own land for your own livelihood, and not simply to put more coins into the pockets of your greedy master, or father, as it were.

Abras takes to farm life most naturally considering he has only picked gold his whole life. He seems to have a deep understanding of the land and works it with great respect.

"He understands tanouli without ever having been taught," Aunt Havita says one afternoon as we watch Abras lovingly coax a spindling bean sprout as if it can understand him. It seems to turn a little greener and stand a little less limply.

He is delighted to discover that, while they had sold the cows, there were a few sheep on the farm, which are sheared for wool in the springtime. One is pregnant, and without hesitation, he asks Aunt Havita if we can name her Elanora.

"What if it's a male?" she asks, laughing.

"What if it is?" he laughs back. "Elanora is a fine name."

And when the lamb is born, a male, Abras is there. "Welcome to the world, Elanora!" he exclaims as he cradles the slippery lamb while the mother recovers.

Sentaya seems content to put in a day of hard work, which Rayon and I find amusing given her childhood propensity to get out of her chores at any cost. She asks only one thing — a riding lesson with Aunt Havita at the end of each day. At first, she just takes a slow ride in circles, but soon she full-on canters up onto the mountain trail. It would seem some parts of her childhood have stuck with Sentaya after all.

Rayon spends his free time exploring the mountain and soon — at Aunt Havita's urging — he takes to writing stories in a bound book that she gives to him. Now, all of his adventures, for so long only a daydream, become words on a page. He reads them to us in the evenings by the fire, and it is not simply our adoration for Rayon that leave us a rapt audience; his stories are surprising and captivating.

To watch Abras, Rayon and Sentaya settle in and find their place on the farm is a great joy. And to come to know Aunt Havita is a most unexpected gift. We sit up many nights telling bits of our stories, now just coming to live side by side even though they should have been intertwined all along.

I tell Aunt Havita about the people we passed in the countryside on our journey here — the hungry children and the mothers, barely older than children themselves. There is a great deal of service needed in the kingdom, and we need to go out and do it.

But despite all of this joy and possibility, the grief for Granna and Teetee sit heavy in my heart.

"It is a grief worse than death, I imagine, because there is no finality to it," Aunt Havita says one night.

"They may very well be out there. That must have been how it was for my parents with Pru."

"The anger is unbearable."

"Ah, yes, the anger," she says knowingly. "Anger is a poison. Who is it that you are angry at?"

"My father. I wanted to destroy him. I thought destroying the mine would cure me of it. But I cannot let it go."

"You sound like me so many years ago; the wind carried away my anger—"

"I wish it were as easy as yelling it into the wind, Aunt Havita," I cut her off. "But I just don't think that the wind is going to help."

"Ah, no, it is not as easy as yelling it into the wind, my love. First, you must make a choice. The wind cannot take it from you; you must choose to give it to it."

"Okay, then I choose to let it go. There, it's gone." I can hear how childish I sound, and I feel my face warm slightly.

But Aunt Havita only smiles sweetly at me, no judgment in her eyes. "You have much to be angry for, Cala. And grief and anger can be tangled together, almost impossible to tell one from the other."

"Well, I don't want any of it!" I yell in exasperation.

"Sadly we do not get to choose what happens to us, only how we respond."

"I did choose. And even though I destroyed the mine, my anger is still intact. There is not enough fire powder in the world to destroy it."

I stomp off, already choking on tears before I reach the door. Abras follows me outside and runs to catch up. He hugs me from behind and holds me until my sobs lessen and I can speak through the tears.

"How can it be that, after everything we've done — after bringing down the mine and getting the slaves out and making it through that impossible journey — that still I cannot find peace?"

"I don't know, Cala. I wish I did."

He holds me a while longer before taking my hand. "Come, let's walk."

We walk hand-in-hand through Granna's meadow until eventually the tears stop altogether. Soon we make our way to the sheep pen and find Elanora snuggled against his mother. We rub his soft wool for a bit before his mother shoos us away from her sleeping babe. Then we snuggle up ourselves amidst the hay, and Abras kisses me slowly until the anger and grief fade.

As night falls, we make our way back to the house, arms around each other's waists.

"Well, screaming into the wind might work fine for anger, but I think I'll take kissing you in a sheep's pen instead," I say.

He laughs. "I help where I'm needed."

As we approach the stone path up to the house, we both slow our gait, hesitant to let these final few moments alone come to an end.

It is then that I see a figure at the end of the path, shadowy in the graying dusk.

"Abras, look," I say, nodding toward the figure. "Who's there?" I call out.

"It is me, sweet girl."

And though she is nothing more than a shadow, Teetee's voice is a beam of light through the darkness, guiding me home.

***

I bury my face into her soft chest and breathe her in. I cling to her, as if it is my very will alone that keeps her from vanishing. And she clings right back, weeping softly into my hair.

"I worried about you every minute," she says through her tears.

"I'm so sorry," I say. "Everything is my fault."

"Hush," she says, stroking my hair. "There is no one to blame but your father, that vile man, sending his own daughter to slave away in that mine. I could kill him."

"I'm okay, Teetee. I'm okay."

Sentaya and Rayon make their way outside, running towards us and then hugging her and gasping.

"What?"

And "How can it be?"

"Teetee, how did you get here?" I ask finally.

She pulls herself away from us and says, "I will tell you everything, but Pru needs our help. We must hurry."

"Pru?" It is Aunt Havita who steps forward now. "Pru is with you?"

"She was, but she couldn't make it any farther. I left her to come get help."

"What? Where?" I ask, my shock turning to disbelief. "Back in Urendia?"

"No, she's here, in Arcalia, but the journey was too much for her. She collapsed in the forest on the outskirts of Galendale. Please, we must go now."

Aunt Havita springs to action. "Abras, help me hitch the wagon. Cala and Sentaya, pack supplies. Rayon, tend to your Teetee. Get her food and water."

Soon, we are scurrying about, readying everything for an uncertain trek back into the woods for Granna. I focus on each task to keep me moving forward. Pump water from the well. Wrap cheese inside a cloth. Pluck apples from a bowl. Anything more would send me spiraling into unanswerable questions and incurable worry.

Sentaya and I emerge back outside as Abras and Aunt Havita pull the hitched wagon up to the front of the house.

"Tetunia, is it?" asks Aunt Havita. "Are you well enough to travel? I'll need you to guide me to Pru."

Teetee nods.

292

"Us," I say. "Guide *us*."

Aunt Havita and Teetee both open their mouths to argue, but they must see something written on my face that stops them: that I have to rescue Granna after she rescued me.

"Abras, Sentaya and Rayon, can I ask you to stay behind and manage the farm? I need you three here," Aunt Havita calls down from the wagon seat.

Abras walks back to me after helping Teetee get into the wagon. "I don't want to say goodbye to you again, Cala," he says, taking me gently by the arms. "What if our luck has run out, and this is our last time?"

I pull him close and whisper into his ear, "Not an earthquake nor a pack of dirawolves nor a swarm of cythas can keep us apart, remember?"

"Nor a raging river nor an abduction by a drunken constable," he adds.

"Nor a rescue mission to bring Granna home," I say finally and kiss him hard before pulling away from him.

"Our list is getting a little long," jokes Abras.

I laugh, grateful as always to Abras for his levity even in the direst of situations. I turn to hug Rayon and Sentaya.

"Be careful," says Sentaya.

***

Teetee gives Aunt Havita direction to set a course then settles back against the wall of the wagon, drooping with exhaustion.

"How did you get here?" I ask. "And how did you connect with Granna?"

"Just let me rest my eyes for a few moments, sweet girl. I will tell you everything, I promise."

She lies down, and even though I am seventeen and taller than Teetee by now, I curl into the space made by her body like I have done so many nights of my life. And as the dark of night swallows our hopeful wagon, I fall asleep to the familiar sounds of Teetee's steady breathing.

***

"There," says Teetee. "That's the trailhead. Pru's down this way."

It is dawn already.

"Are we near Granna?" I call out.

"I think so," says Teetee. "I don't remember walking much farther from where I left Pru before I got to the main road. I tied my scarf around the tree to signal where to turn into the brush to find her."

I sit up on my knees, peering over the side of the wagon and scanning the trees for a scarf. We are each lost in our own search, and perhaps our own thoughts, as we continue down the forest path.

Granna has come to mean something very different to each of us. For me, a lifeline, a source of love and comfort when the misery of the mine might have destroyed me altogether.

For Aunt Havita, a long-lost sister, the missing piece to her broken family, now finally, hopefully, coming home.

And for Teetee, well, I'm not entirely sure what Granna is to Teetee. I open my mouth to resume my line of questioning from the night before when suddenly Teetee shouts out, "There!"

I follow her outstretched finger to see a deep red scarf, one that she wore tied around her head many days from my childhood, now tied to a tree and fluttering in the breeze, as if to wave us toward Granna.

Aunt Havita stops the wagon and we all hop down, cutting into the brush in search of Pru.

"I left her here," says Teetee, leading us further into the thicket.

Soon, I see what appears to be a clump of brown rags dropped in front of a tree, but as I get closer, I see that it is Granna, slumped over.

Aunt Havita rushes to her and puts her head to her chest. "She is still breathing, but just barely. We need to get her back."

We circle around Granna to lift her. She hardly weighs anything, and we carry her easily to the back of the wagon.

"I will stay back here with Pru," says Aunt Havita. "I need to rest after driving all night. Can the two of you manage with the wagon."

"I think so," I say.

"Yes," says Teetee confidently. "I've driven a wagon before."

I stare at her searchingly then remember that Teetee led a secret life all those years and very well may have a whole host of skills that go beyond house chores.

I climb onto the driver's seat next to Teetee as she takes the reins and turns us back toward home. She settles the horse into a steady trot before she turns to me and says, "Now then, I think I owe you a story."

***

"I spent those first days — or weeks, I'm not sure — in a cell in the castle dungeon. They wanted me to tell them where I was in those hours that your father waited for me in our bedroom. They were quite determined. I don't want to talk much more about those days."

"I'm so sorry, Teetee. I wish I hadn't written that letter."

"It would have happened one way or another, Cala. I take pride in knowing that it happened because you stood up for yourself."

I consider that a moment. "It just seemed so foolish."

"It was foolish, sweet girl, but it was foolish for the right reason, and that is something." She turns toward me to smile reassuringly before continuing on. "So eventually, when they realized they wouldn't get anything out of me, they put me in a prisoners' wagon with a few others and sent me to the countryside to carry out my sentence: ten years of hard labor. I begged them to take me to the mine, but of course, they wouldn't. Your father would not give us that.

"Finally, we reached the camps where prisoners are held and farmers can come to request labor. When the farmer walked in and looked at me, he pointed and said, 'I'll take that one'. I knew then that things weren't going to get much better for me."

"Granna said some of the farmers treated the workers kindly," I interject. "I hoped and hoped that that would be true for you."

"It was not," she replies flatly. "But lucky for me, I was no stranger to cruel men, and I understood that the best way is to give them what they want: deference. At their core, cruel men are really just weak, Cala."

"What did he do?" I ask, uncertain that I really wanted to know.

"Oh, he worked us too hard and didn't feed us enough and chained our ankles at night so we couldn't escape." She lifts her tunic to show me the still-healing wounds around her ankles.

I suck air in through my teeth reflexively at the sight of Teetee's raw ankles.

"I won't get into the rest. But I knew The Servants would find me and help me. And soon, they did. The farmer hired a driver to come take his crop to market. Somehow, The Servants got to the driver and began to send word."

"Their reach really seems to have no end," I marvel.

"Indeed, The Servants are extraordinary in their ways. The first note that came said that you were safe in the mine, and a plan was underway. The next said a placement was being arranged and to await further detail. But then, that was it. I never got any further word. That's when things took a turn for me. I was overcome with worry for you and the plan and uncertain about my own fate. The Servants knew where I was, so I didn't feel that I could leave as it might mean losing contact with you altogether. I felt trapped, and that was very difficult to bear."

She pauses for some time, lost in some memory that she does not share.

"But then," she starts again suddenly. "A most unexpected thing happened. Another wagon of workers arrived, and with them, an older woman. Soon we got to talking and realized that you were this precious bond between us. I felt as if a miracle was unfolding right before me.

"She told me the whole story of your plan and how you saw it through. I was so proud, Cala, hearing what you did. And then, she told me of the escape and what she did to save you. And I was overcome with gratitude for this woman. Apparently, when the mine was destroyed, they didn't have anywhere to put her, so they sent her to labor in the countryside."

"I thought they would send her straight to the gallows, hold her responsible for everything. I don't understand."

"Onaris took the fall, Cala. He said that it was his plan, and his alone. Given his high profile with The Servants, they seemed to believe him. The execution was swift."

Grief and guilt mix to form bitter tears. "But it was my plan. I should have been the one."

"Cala, Onaris died doing what he lived for: serving others. I knew him well during my time with The Servants. Believe me when I tell you, living to be an old man and dying to save you, Pru, and all the other slaves, it would have been a death that he welcomed. It is a great loss, but a noble one."

Teetee takes my hand in hers and pauses her story awhile, leaving me to my grief.

Eventually she goes on. "Pru was better than a final note from The Servants. She was a living map. I could leave because I knew where to find you. As the farmer shackled us that last night, Pru distracted him while I took him out from behind with an iron hoe. It was a most satisfying blow.

"I knew how to get us to the Arcalian border, and from there, Pru could guide us here. But it was too much for her. We encountered some bad weather followed by a cold night, and I think it settled into her lungs. She had more and more trouble breathing until finally she couldn't go on. She said to leave her and go get help. So that's what I did."

"It all just seems so improbable."

"The whole thing is. What you pulled off in the mine. I can't even fathom all that had to go right in order for us to be sitting here this very moment talking to each other. You and I have had our fair share of pain, Cala, but this life has given us a great many gifts as well."

I think of laughing with my siblings and curling up to Granna in the mine and kissing Abras and Aunt Havita sharing her story with me and sitting right here beside Teetee on this rickety wagon. "It has given us a great many gifts indeed."

We ride in silence for some time, taking in the gravity of all that has happened to bring us back together. And then, from the back of the wagon, we hear Aunt Havita call with urgency, "Her breathing is getting slower, we must hurry."

***

The others have gone to bed, having spent their time hovered around Granna's sick bed, whispering whatever words they needed to say.

Now just Aunt Havita, Abras and I remain, watching her chest rise and fall slowly as a rattling sound comes from her lungs. Aunt Havita has done what she can, mixing a poultice and spreading it onto Granna's chest and making a concoction of herbs that she brewed into a tea. She said that it is up to Granna now.

I think of Granna in the mine — so strong and assured despite her age — and I cannot think of any other outcome than her popping up out of bed and giving us one of her winks.

But now, she is this frail thing with a rattling breath.

Suddenly her eyes flutter open and fix on me. "Cala, you are safe."

My heart takes flight.

"I am safe, Granna."

Her eyes wander over to Abras. "Abras," she wheezes. "You, too."

"Yes, Pru. And so are you. We all made it here, to your home."

"My home," she repeats back, closing her eyes as if focusing all her attention on the feeling of home.

"And there's more, Granna," I say.

She opens her eyes again.

"This is Havita, your sister." I nod over to Havita across from us on the other side of the bed.

Granna shifts her head slightly and looks over to Havita.

"My sister. You are beautiful." Tears begin to form in both of their eyes as they take each other in.

"I am so happy to meet you, Pru," says Havita. "Our family was never complete without you."

"I hoped that they could move on," Granna says between breaths.

"They found peace by the end," says Havita. "But losing you was something they could never get past."

They are quiet for some time, grieving the life that was taken from them.

"Please take care of each other," Granna says faintly after some time.

"No, Granna," I say, pleading, crying. "You made it home. We can all take care of each other now."

"My body is spent, my child."

"No, please, you just need to be strong a little longer. You can live, free now."

"You... both of you," she glances toward me and Abras. "You gave me a family. You made it a life. I was free all along." She erupts into a fit of coughing, and I can see how difficult it is for her to talk, to breathe even.

I am bent over her, crying. "I don't want you to go."

"Hush, hush," she whispers. Then her eyes close, and she drifts back to sleep.

Her breathing grows slower and more ragged until eventually it stops altogether.

Aunt Havita comes over and holds us both. "She died in peace, in her home," she says. "You gave her that. What an extraordinary gift."

"She gave us many gifts over the years," says Abras.

"Goodbye, Granna," I whisper at last.

**

We bury Granna next to her parents, and the rightness of that softens our grief.

We tell stories of Granna, and Teetee tells us of her time with Granna, from when she arrived at the farm to their journey home.

"She wasn't on the farm long before we escaped, but in the little time that she was there, she showed such care for the other workers. As soon as she saw the shackles and our raw ankles, she set about making a salve from what she could find. She rubbed it on each and every ankle with such loving hands. You would think we were her closest of kin, not mere strangers."

We all offer our own stories of Granna's healing and protection, how she'd patch us up and steel us to carry on for one more day.

"I wish I had gotten to know her," says Aunt Havita. "But from what you are all describing, it sounds very much like Pru's kimbasa may have been an anterlope as well, protective and maternal. Even though we spent our lives a kingdom apart, I think we shared a very special connection."

We smile through our tears for Aunt Havita as she manages to salvage something from their life of loss.

When the day comes to an end, we sit together, taking in the warmth of the fire and each other's company. And somehow the heaviness at losing Granna sits in my heart right alongside a great lightness for what surrounds me: my family and the start of our new story.

But then, at some point in the night, I notice Aunt Havita slip out to steal up to the mountain.

Chapter 18
Havita

After we bury Pru, I leave the others to make my way up to the mountain, and this time, it is in anger — hot, dizzying, tearful anger.

It was difficult to bear the loss of my father, but this was entirely another thing. Now I have to bear the loss of someone who I never even expected to know?

In those few hours with her, I began to envision a future, one where my sister would be alive and here with me, holding my hand and calling me beautiful, but that vision vanished with her last rattling breaths.

The unfairness of it all rips through me and leaves me seething in its wake.

But before I can make it beyond the meadow, a voice calls from behind me.

"Aunt Havita, wait!" Cala calls from behind me.

It is effortful to pull myself from my rage, already beginning to sweep me away, but when Cala softly touches my shoulder, she pulls me back.

"You don't have to do this alone, Aunt Havita."

"It's the only way I know."

"We're here now. Could you learn a different way?"

"I don't know," I say. And then, after sometime, "Maybe I could try."

She loops her arm around my shoulder and we turn back toward the house.

The house is alight — brimming with warmth made by the very people that Pru led here. She may have been a fleeting presence, but the family that she brought together is just beginning its story.

**

In the late hours of the night — the fire nothing but glowing embers — only Tetunia and I are still awake.

"After your journey, you must be exhausted. Can I show you to your bed?" I ask.

"In a moment," Tetunia says. I wanted to see that you were all right."

"Huh," I respond. "It has been a good long while since anyone has asked me that."

"Oh," she said. "Well, are you all right?"

"No, not really," I say, settling into the chair next to her.

"I can't imagine how you could be."

"Are you all right?" I ask her.

"No, not really," she says.

"Well good, we've got that settled." And we both laugh, kicking up the layers of grief that have settled one upon another.

We stay up long into the night, sharing the ways we have not been all right.

But as the first rays of dawn pierce through the night, our conversation turns to a way forward — a chance to build a life not weighed down by an oppressive man or a grief-stricken mother or anger that is poison, but one of joy and hope and love. We are entranced by the possibility of it.

"Cala is bent on bringing The Servants here," Tetunia says at one point.

"It is a noble cause," I say truthfully.

"I understand that you might be hesitant to consider such a thing."

"It is nothing against The Servants. Based on what they accomplished in the mines alone, it seems like a most impressive organization."

"What is it, then?"

"A need to protect what I have built, I suppose. Pru's Place has served the good people of this village — and beyond — while staying discreet. The king may not be as heartless as his father and his Offering, but I do not wish to provoke his ire."

"It's a risk. I know that as much as anyone."

"And yet, you would assume such a risk again?" I ask. "Even after everything you have endured?"

Tetunia sighs heavily at that. "Existing in this world without working to make it better does not seem like a worthwhile existence to me. Becoming a Servant was the first time that my life mattered."

"I feel the same about Pru's Place."

"You have made an important contribution, Havita. I hope you do not feel that we don't see that."

"Give me some time with the idea," I say finally.

"Of course," she says. "Take all the time you need." With that she stands, stretching. "And now, my exhaustion truly is heavy."

"Rest well, Tetunia."

As she turns to leave, a thought occurs to me. "You know, today I lost a sister, and the unfairness of it left me spinning. But tonight, I believe I may have discovered a sister, and for that, I am truly grateful."

"As am I, Havita." And I can hear that she is smiling. "As am I."

***

Later in the season, Cala and I find ourselves in the city, bringing some of the farm's vegetable harvest to market. We supply a woman — Dalian — who has a stall there and who trained at Pru's Place some years ago. Many of the surrounding farms supply sellers with a heavy profit built in. I do my best to offer her a fair price.

"Your tomatoes are looking especially beautiful today, Havita."

"Thank you, Dali! Abras has us planting them next to the amaranth now, and it keeps the bugs off wondrously."

"He sure does seem to have a knack for farm life."

"It's been a joy to watch. How's business been?"

"It's been good, Havita, no small thanks to you."

Just then a young boy approaches us. He looks up at me with sullen brown eyes. "Could you spare a coin, miss?"

"Of course," I say, dropping a coin into his outstretched hand. "You know, I was just about to find some lunch before I head back to my village. Could I persuade you to join me?"

He turns around to look behind him for a moment, then faces me, now fear clearly registering in his eyes.

"I better not, miss," he says, as he walks away, shoulders slumped.

"Likely returning to his master," Dalian says. "Many such children in this city do their begging — sometimes worse — under the watchful eye of a master. They turn over everything they make with no reward."

"I have heard of such things, but to see it, how awful," I say, watching his small figure disappear into the streets beyond the market.

***

Later, on the way home, as Cala chatters on about newly purchased fabric, my mind wanders back to the boy from the marketplace. The sullen and then fearful look on his face. His tattered clothes and shoeless feet. The bent over way that he carried himself, as if the weight of his troubles were too much for his small body to bear.

I feel desperate to rescue him, to stow him away in our wagon, now emptied of the vegetables, and to take him home to our farm, where his life would be good. But then I think of what Dalian said, that there were many such children in the city suffering the same fate — even worse — and I realize that even if I could find him and bear him home, there would be countless other children who couldn't be helped.

"Maybe this one will work well for our tunics," Cala says, holding up a deep purple fabric. "What do you think, Aunt Havita?"

"I think I am ready to talk more about The Servants."

Chapter 19
Cala

We worked the farm through harvest time, and then winter descended and we got to join Aunt Havita's wintertime students. We all have much to learn, and we studied and trained right alongside the girls, even Rayon.

As winter — and training time — came to an end, we spent what little extra time we had planning the work of The Servants. With Teetee's experience and Aunt Havita's existing connections, we were well on our way. But we knew we would need more than our small group, determined as we were, if we were going to make any real difference.

And so, we began to travel our village and the nearby ones as well, talking to friends of Aunt Havita's, and eventually friends of friends. It was a delicate dance, testing out interest without revealing too much lest someone might share our plans with the authorities. But slowly, person by person, we passed along our message: if you are committed to serving the good people of Arcalia, join us at Pru's Place on the first full moon of spring.

***

On the night of the meeting, while Aunt Havita and Sentaya busy themselves preparing a spread of food, Teetee and Rayon are camped out at the end of the stone path, keeping watch for anyone who might wish to do us harm.

Abras stands beside me in the barn, his arm around my waist.

"What if they don't come?" I allow myself to wonder aloud. "What if they don't want to follow me."

"They will follow you," he reassures me. "Your mother knew that you were the first rays at dawn, the start of a new day. They will follow you."

And even though uncertainty twists in my stomach, I believe him. This does feel like the start. I will serve the people of Arcalia in any way that I can. How else can I earn the debt that Onaris and Granna have paid? How else can I live out my mother's and my grandfather's mission, the one that Teetee nearly died carrying on?

This story of mine will have pain, to be certain. But it will have joy, too. And both will dwell in my heart, side by side, like sun and shadow.

And then, the barn door opens, and our neighboring farmer and his two daughters arrive. They nod to me and take their seats. From there, the stream of people is steady. An old man from a neighboring village. A widow and her son from the town over. Even the old lady who sells honey by the side of the road and has only ever scowled at us, even when we bought her honey by the jarful.

Soon, the seats are full and people begin to stand around the edge of the barn, finding room where they can. They look up toward the front, toward me, standing on a box facing out at them. My family — here despite so many odds against them — sits in the front row. I take a deep, steadying breath and begin.

"My name is Calandria Cida." I gaze down at Abras, beaming back up at me. "And on behalf of my family—the ones sitting here today and the ones who are here only in our hearts—I now call to order the first meeting of the Servants of Arcalia."